Scruffy and the Secret Life of the Queen

Scruffy

and the Secret Life of

the Queen

EWAN PETTMAN

This is a work of fiction. Any similarities to real persons or events are purely coincidental. In some cases, as coincidental as possible without actually being facts.

For my middle orange

Contents

Chapter 1

'One does love a good pizza!' said the Queen to herself. She never really refers to herself as 'one', of course, that's just one of those things that everyone thinks but is actually not true at all. Except for when she's in her secret bungalow, where she goes when she needs a break from all the reigning that she does.

She was just settling down to watch *EastEnders* when her pizza arrived. It had her favourite toppings: chopped Mars bar, anchovies, and plenty of chilli sauce. The Queen's love of pizza is a closely kept secret, and the only time she eats pizza is when she's very happy.

Her secret bungalow is in Craystead, in the corner of London that old-fashioned people still call Surrey. The bungalow has shabby carpets that might make you giddy if you stare at them, and wallpaper that looks like it could make you sneeze. There's a trampoline in the back garden, although the Queen hasn't done star jumps on it since 1987. There's a tall privet hedge around the secret bungalow, to give the Queen privacy. She wouldn't want to be recognized by anyone in Craystead, so whenever she goes in or out of her bungalow she wears a black patch over her left eye.

It was a fine Tuesday evening in late July. Earlier, the Queen had enjoyed a pleasant meeting with Mr Major, the Prime Minister. You might think these meetings are about important government matters, but the Queen doesn't get involved in politics. Whenever she meets a politician in private, they play snakes and ladders. That day, she won two games out of three. As a forfeit, she made the Prime Minister stand on his head for twenty minutes while balancing one of her pinkest hats on his feet. He'd made her do some terrible forfeits whenever she'd lost at snakes and ladders.

Prince Philip was abroad on navy business, the Queen Mother was at Goodwood for the races, and Prince Charles had taken Princes William and Harry on a royal tour of Africa. The Queen had received a postcard from young Prince Harry, with a photo of a chimpanzee wearing a frilly blue dress, a necklace made of shiny orange pebbles, and a hat that looked like an ice-cream sundae. The chimpanzee had a cheeky grin and was waving with one hand. On the back of the card Harry had written, 'I saw this picture and it reminded me of you!'

With the family away, the Queen could relax in her secret bungalow and pretend she was just like any other grandmother. Buckingham Palace is alright, but there's nothing the Queen loves more than baking and knitting, although she isn't very good at either of these activities.

She once baked a cake containing her favourite pizza toppings. The chopped Mars bars made the cake fabulously gooey in the parts that were edible, but there were far too many anchovies. She included diced cucumbers in the mixture, in an attempt to offset the saltiness of the anchovies, but this made the cake all soggy. She did feel that mixing chilli sauce into the icing gave a magically exotic flavour, but nobody else agreed. When Prince Philip took a bite, his face turned a bright shade of purple and his hair stuck out in several directions.

Another time, the Queen knitted a pair of socks for Prince Charles, but one sock was much larger than the other, and neither would fit his feet. Not wishing to disappoint his mother, that winter Charles insisted on wearing the socks on his ears to keep them warm during a skiing trip, but only when out of sight of any photographers.

During this retreat to her secret bungalow, the Queen decided not to indulge her creative side, and instead to read some of the government papers that are often sent to her for perusal. Sometimes she looks at the fun ones.

There was a proposal to develop a vaccine against grumpiness. The Queen considered that an excellent idea, but she couldn't imagine Mr Major supporting it. Another idea was to clean up the streets by soaking sheep in Fairy liquid and marching them through the UK's towns and cities.

A proposal she was quite keen on was to give all schoolchildren doughnuts with their school dinners, but the jam inside would be made from broccoli and cabbage, to make it healthy. When Prince Charles was a boy, the Queen once made him a doughnut just like that, and when he ate it he grinned like a cat that had caught a six-legged mouse.

The Queen suspected that none of these could ever happen, but she was amused by them. There were, however, some more pressing matters on the Queen's mind.

As *EastEnders* was finishing, she took another slice of pizza, and thought about a suggestion from one of her aides, to boost her popularity by finding a stray dog to adopt as a new playmate for her corgis. 'The newspapers would love it, but would the corgis?' she mused to herself.

When she can spend time in her secret bungalow, the Queen relishes pretending to be a commoner, but she cannot do this often, and in any other setting she would never be seen eating pizza or knitting wonky socks. Would making friends with an untidy mutt be fitting for a monarch? She would have to give it some thought, but for now she would finish her pizza, and spend some time daydreaming about life as an ordinary grandmother, before going to bed early.

*   *   *

'I do love a good cheese scone!' Granny proclaimed. Robert and his grandmother were sitting in the sunshine in the garden of her little house in Craystead, while Granny's beloved dog Scruffy busily tossed sticks and dug small holes in the garden, which didn't annoy Granny as much as it used to.

'I prefer the fruit scones,' Robert said, 'they're sweeter.'

'But you're eating yours with cheese and ketchup,' Granny replied.

'You might think that's odd, Granny, but you always put silly things on your scones!'

'I'm having the same on my scone as I always have,' Granny retorted, 'some slices of Mars bar, an anchovy, and a good dollop of chilli sauce. Nothing silly about that.'

Robert turned up his nose and said, 'Yuck.'

That morning Robert and Granny had been to the hairdresser. Robert hated having his hair cut, and he didn't see the point of anything so boring so early in the summer holidays. His red hair was always a mess even after a trim, but Granny loved being neat. She always wore a brightly coloured cardigan and a blouse dotted with little flowers, and took pride in her white hair neatly pruned into tight curls, which Robert thought made her head look like a cauliflower. Her skin was as wrinkled as a cabbage, but she was no vegetable. Her mind was as sharp as a spade.

Scruffy was messier than any animal you've ever seen. Nobody was quite sure what kind of dog Scruffy was, but his small size, and the colour of his scraggly coat, were close to Yorkshire terrier. Once, Scruffy was taken to see a groomer, and Scruffy was so angry that he wrestled a bottle of doggy shampoo from the groomer's hands, jumped through a window, and buried the shampoo under a tangled prickly bush. That was the last time anyone dared to do anything about Scruffy's appearance. Scruffy was cheerful and friendly with a tail that waggled like an old duster, but woe betide anyone going near him with a brush or a comb.

'I'm going to play with my helicopter,' Robert announced, after he ate the last bite of his scone. Granny had bought him a toy helicopter on their way back from the hairdresser. It was the kind that takes off when you pull a cord, soaring rapidly into the air, just like the real thing.

'Be careful not to make it fly too far!' Granny warned, 'You wouldn't want it going over the fence.'

But before Granny finished speaking, Robert pulled the cord with as much force as he could, sending the toy flying high like a plastic eagle, then plonking down in the middle of next door's garden.

'You'll have to go and knock on Mrs Gibbons's door and ask for that back,' Granny told Robert, with a look that said she'd warned him.

Robert felt awkward for a moment, and hesitated. 'I'll go and ask for it back soon, Granny, just let me think about it first. I'm a bit nervous.'

'There's nothing to be scared of,' Granny insisted. 'I know Mrs Gibbons dresses up as a witch sometimes, but that's only because she goes to a lot of fancy dress parties. I know you saw Mrs Gibbons carrying an axe once, but she said the red marks on it were just paint, and she was only going to help someone chop down a tree. And I know Mrs Gibbons shouted at you before, but she was having a bad day, her cat had just gone missing. I'm sure she's lovely once you get to know her.'

'Let me wait a few minutes first,' Robert answered, his lower lip quivering slightly. Granny had a feeling she would eventually have to go next door to recover the helicopter herself.

Robert was staying with Granny for two weeks of the summer holidays while his parents were recovering from the most curious accident, which Granny had witnessed.

The accident happened like this. Granny had taken Scruffy to the park with Robert's parents, and had just scolded Scruffy for fiercely bothering a seagull, which had stolen a biscuit from Granny. Turning towards a bench where Robert's mum and dad were sitting, Granny saw a smartly dressed lady fall out of a tree, landing right on top of the couple.

It turned out that the smartly dressed lady was wearing a pair of earrings made of hazelnuts, and a squirrel had climbed up to the lady's shoulders, so quietly and gently that this went unnoticed until the squirrel yanked one of the hazelnut earrings into his greedy paws. With narrowed eyes, the lady watched the squirrel climb high into the tree, and then she clambered up the branches in pursuit, only to lose her footing and tumble when she took her earring back.

Both parents were fine, but shaken by the experience. So, Granny arranged for them to go on a yoga retreat, where they would learn to relax and try out some bizarre yoga positions, such as the magnificent Beached Octopus pose. Soon, Robert and Granny would have something else to worry about.

'Oh look, Robert, Scruffy's got that big beef bone!' Granny said. 'I thought he'd lost it. He must've buried it ages ago — he has been digging in my lawn more often lately — now he's found it. It's amazing how a little dog like Scruffy can handle such a heavy bone!'

Granny stood up and went inside to get another scone, and Robert watched as Scruffy growled, struggling to pull the bone out from beneath the grass, then Robert followed Granny into the house, still nervously thinking about his helicopter.

A moment later, another dog squeezed his way through a gap in Granny's fence, shook some dry mud off his matted fur, and ran to Scruffy, sweeping the bone from his surprised jaws. Scruffy let out a howl, then a fit of violent barking so loud that every bird nearby shot into the sky like a twittering explosion.

Robert and Granny looked through the kitchen window, but it was too late for them to act. The intruding beast leapt on to Granny's coal bunker, from there to the roof of the shed, then over the fence and out of sight. Scruffy dashed right after him.

Granny glanced at Robert, Robert glanced at Granny, then Robert scurried to the back gate. Granny followed him as quickly as she could. They were out of luck. Scruffy, and the stray dog bone thief, were nowhere to be seen.

'Maybe we should ask Mrs Gibbons next door if she'll help us look for him,' Granny whimpered.

'I'm sure we'll find him ourselves,' Robert replied. 'How far could he go?'

Chapter 2

'I do love a well-polished garden gnome!' Mrs Pittick said to her son, Arnold, who, as usual, was doing something revolting, while she was tidying their front lawn.

Looking up, Arnold saw Robert and his granny, who appeared flustered. The pair had been frantically searching for Scruffy in every road and every alleyway around their home in Craystead, but so far had not seen a whisker of him, nor heard a single bark. They even had some help from a pizza delivery man, who drove them around for fifteen minutes as they gazed into every nook and cranny, before he had to return to the takeaway to collect a pizza for the secretive posh lady in the bungalow with the tall privet hedge.

Arnold called out, 'Hey, Robert, look at this!'

'What are you doing with a dolls' house in the garden, Arnold?' Robert asked.

'It's a very dirty dolls' house, it smells like a compost heap,' Granny remarked.

Arnold sighed, 'Of course it's dirty, my dad found it in a skip! Now it's a palace for earthworms. Look, these worms are having their dinner. I gave them some dandelions and dead spiders to eat. These worms upstairs are taking a bath together, and these worms in the bedroom are trying to get some sleep, but they're wriggling around an awful lot, must be having bad dreams.'

Robert wished he hadn't asked.

'Don't worry about him,' Mrs Pittick interrupted, 'Arnold used to hate helping his dad collect worms for fishing. This way he loves it. How are your parents after last week's accident, Robert?'

'Oh, they're fine. They've gone on a yoga retreat to steady their nerves. We're more worried about Scruffy right now,' Robert answered.

'Sounds wonderful,' Mrs Pittick said. 'Yoga's great. I've been doing a lot of Beached Octopus pose lately.'

'Ah yes, Beached Octopus, that's a magnificent yoga pose!' said Granny.

Robert was getting agitated and his face was beginning to turn pink. All he could think about was finding Scruffy.

Mrs Pittick went on, 'I wish Arnold didn't find yoga boring. He'd be so good at it. He's double jointed.'

Robert had heard enough of this. 'But what about Scruffy? He's missing!'

Just then there was a loud brrrppp behind him, it was the sound of Sam's bicycle brakes. Sam was a curly-haired boy from Robert's class in school. They used to sit together in lessons, until one day they got caught flicking tiny bits of paper into a girl's hair during a really dull spelling test. After that, the teacher made them sit where they couldn't distract each other.

'Scruffy's missing?' Sam asked.

'Yes,' replied Robert, 'a big ugly dog stole his bone and Scruffy ran away.'

'He'll be fine,' Sam said dismissively, 'Arnold, do that trick with your hands.'

Arnold pressed his grubby hands together, turned them upside down, and bent his wrists backwards in a way that's impossible for everybody else.

'Cor, that's disgusting!' Sam laughed, 'It makes me feel sick when you do that.'

Robert wasn't impressed, his one concern was the whereabouts of Scruffy, and he was exasperated with the lack of sympathy from his friends. In frustration, his face went almost as red as his hair.

Granny said, 'Nice trick, lad, but listen. Scruffy's never run away before. He has no sense of direction. He sees squirrels and he runs towards them, and when he's had too many biscuits he chases his tail. Apart from that, he never knows where he's going.'

'I'll help you look,' said Sam.

'So will I,' said Arnold, pulling some mud out of his greasy blond hair, 'but why don't you just put some posters up?'

'Well, that might sound like a good plan,' Granny answered, 'but posters are no good, it'll take ages, you just don't know how far away Scruffy could get while we're choosing a picture and getting photocopies. Besides, there are always loads of posters around here for lost cats. Don't know where those cats go, but they're never found. Let's keep looking, we'll find him.'

'Is your phone number on his collar?' Mrs Pittick asked.

Granny looked at the ground. 'Well, it was,' she explained, 'but Robert found the tag with my phone number on, it was snagged on the fence. Let's hope he's still wearing his collar and name tag.'

'Hey, Robert, if you can't find Scruffy, you'll have to start doing your homework,' Sam joked, but Robert didn't understand. 'You remember, a few weeks ago you said Scruffy ate your maths homework. No way the teacher believed you.'

'Scruffy did eat Robert's homework,' Granny asserted, 'Robert spent ages on his long division, then he put it on the floor and Scruffy wolfed it down. I should've given him his dinner before our visit.'

'Remember when I pulled a massive bogey out of my nose and fed it to him?' Arnold exclaimed. 'He gobbled it up and started licking my nose looking for more.'

'It should be Arnold's bedtime soon,' Mrs Pittick said. 'If you're going to form a Scruffy search party, do it now. Arnold, you get back here in one hour, and don't be late. Best of luck, all four of you!'

* * *

Scruffy was not far away. The stray with Scruffy's bone had a head start, but Scruffy's keen sense of smell showed him where to go. He went around one corner, then around another, through some bushes, up a narrow lane — and then he saw it! His beloved bone, hanging like a lopsided medal from the stray dog's jaws.

Scruffy licked his lips and was about to run straight for the prize, but at that moment he squeaked in shock, as he was lifted from the ground by a lady he'd never met before. There was a strong smell of cats.

Scruffy, like most dogs, would normally bark at the slightest hint of threat or excitement, but when truly frightened his normal reaction was to freeze and fall completely silent, as if playing dead. This was one of those moments.

'Aren't you a lovely pussy!' the lady chirped with a smile. 'I bet you're a pretty pussy too, it's such a shame my eyesight is so poor,' she added. Scruffy was about the same size as the average cat, so it was an easy mistake to make for a short-sighted person without the aid of spectacles.

Scruffy managed a quiet growl, and the lady squawked, 'That's the most unusual purr I've ever heard! My name's Doris, and I'm taking you inside to meet your new brothers and sisters. You don't smell like a normal moggy, it's bath time for you.'

Bewildered, Scruffy remained quiet as Doris carried him in her arms like a baby. Entering her house, she dumped Scruffy in the living room and shut the door behind him. 'I'm going to run your bath!' she screeched as she went up the stairs, and on her way she thought to herself, 'That's funny. Very loud barking outside. If I didn't know better, I'd think there's a dog in my home.'

Scruffy was the one barking. Everywhere he looked, he was surrounded by cats. He jumped at one cat and ran in circles with another. He chased one more across a table, knocking over a lamp and a pile of video cassettes, which collided with three cats cowering beneath a chair. When they jumped up, the chair toppled and smashed a vase.

Now in the middle of the room, Scruffy was spoilt for choice, and hesitated, wondering which cat to go for next. Glancing at each other in the way that only felines do, Scruffy's opponents took this moment to gang up on him, forming a ring around Scruffy. Some of them bared their claws and hissed. Scruffy fell silent again and kept still, shaking a little.

'Bath's ready!' Doris announced triumphantly, throwing the door wide open. The cats scattered as she picked up Scruffy. Oblivious to the mess, she took him up to the bathroom, Scruffy still in stunned silence as the smell of soap grew stronger. Throwing him into the bathtub, Doris picked up a brush and leaned towards him. Now Scruffy came to his senses and found his voice. He leapt out of the bath and barked as violently as he could.

'How dare you pretend to be a cat!' Doris shrieked. 'Get out of my house you horrible dog!' She rushed to the front door, and Scruffy was glad to be released.

The stray with Scruffy's bone was long gone, but, sniffing the ground, Scruffy knew which way to go. He shook the awful bathwater out of his coat, and trotted in the direction of the stray dog and the succulent beef bone.

* * *

'Well, that's an idea!' the Queen exclaimed sarcastically. 'Do you really think I'd look good dressed as a monkey?' This was a few days earlier, when the Queen held a meeting with the cleverest staff in Buckingham Palace, to discuss ways to make her more popular.

The newspapers had been giving the Queen a hard time for months. It all began when someone left the lights on in Windsor Castle, which started a fire. Nobody would own up to it, the whole Royal Family argued about who started the fire, and some of the princes and princesses stopped speaking to each other. This made the newspapers rather unhappy, because they wanted photos of smiling royals having fun together. The Queen needed a publicity stunt to cheer everybody up.

So, she gathered all her favourite servants together, and asked them for ideas. It was the royal vet who suggested she dress up as a monkey for a tour of London Zoo.

'Ma'am, I realize dressing up as a monkey isn't all that regal,' said the vet, 'but if Your Majesty wears a crown at all times it will be obvious that Your Majesty is not actually a monkey. Like a king of the jungle, but one of the people, both at the same time.'

The Queen's face looked like she had just choked on an elephant. 'Preposterous,' she croaked. Taking a deep breath, she calmed down and said, 'Perhaps something that doesn't involve me putting on a silly outfit?'

The cook had a completely different plan. 'How about asking the BBC to start a new talent show? Your Majesty will be the host. Each week, the contestants will perform scenes from pantomimes, and the viewers will vote for their favourite. The winner will be proclaimed a royal prince or princess!'

'That's a good one,' said the royal vet, 'we could call it *The People's Princess.*'

'I don't like that,' the cook said, 'they'll be doing pantomime scenes, so what about *Fun 'n' Dames*?'

The Queen's eyes rolled like snooker balls, and she shook her head in pretend disbelief. She secretly quite liked the idea, but wouldn't admit it. 'That's almost as ghastly as the monkey costume, and it might break several laws, surely someone can do better?'

The polisher of the royal shoes remarked that a lot of people were interested in UFOs, and suggested the Queen make a speech on live television, inviting any aliens watching the broadcast to come to Buckingham Palace for afternoon tea. The Queen thought that was ridiculous too, and her eyes looked like they could burst.

'That gives me an idea!' said the head butler, 'How about Your Majesty goes into space? The first queen in space, the whole world will be pleased!'

The Queen imagined herself in a spaceship, floating silently and gently, looking down on all her favourite places from high above. Britain. Malta. The Cayman Islands. Australia. Then she pictured herself travelling to the moon in the spacecraft, watching *EastEnders* on a little round screen, and eating lots and lots of pizza. She wondered whether astronauts can eat pizza in space. Then she remembered that astronauts have to eat horrible dried food, squeezing it out of a tube, just like toothpaste. She didn't think dried toothpaste pizza would be as tasty as what she could eat on Earth.

'No, I don't think so,' she answered, thoughtfully.

The royal vet piped up again, 'OK, so the monkey costume was a bad idea, but everyone loves animals. What about picking up a stray dog from the streets, and giving him a new home with the royal corgis? Your Majesty could give him a throne made of dog biscuits, and throw him sticks made of gold.'

'Not sure about the gold sticks,' the Queen replied, 'but at least that's sensible.' She looked at her watch and saw the time. The Queen did not want to miss the next episode of *Neighbours*. 'Lots for me to think about,' she said. 'Now I have some extremely important royal business that needs my attention, so it's time to go.' The Queen didn't feel the meeting was especially productive, but she is a lover of dogs, so there was one good idea for her to consider. 'I wonder where that might lead,' she mused to herself as she wandered out of the room.

Chapter 3

'I do love a stolen sausage!' Ron said to his two brothers, enjoying a barbecue in the sunshine. 'Especially with a good dollop of chocolate sauce!' The gangsters called themselves the Craystead Four, but there were only three of them. They were no good at maths, but that wasn't the reason for their choice of name. As the Craystead Four, they believed that whenever they were caught and imprisoned, the police would waste time hunting the non-existent fourth member of the gang.

Don, Ron, and Con thought they were pretty clever, but the police nicknamed them the Three Idiots. Always leaving clues at the scenes of their crimes, the careless brothers had been in prison more times than the Queen has eaten pizza.

When they were boys, they broke into a posh school in Kingston upon Thames, and stole all the chalk from the classrooms, so the teachers couldn't write on the blackboards. Then, they tried to sell the stolen chalk to the headmaster of their own school in Craystead. They were promptly expelled and sent to a horrible boarding school for nasty children, where school dinners were always cauliflower and sprout stew, which the dinner ladies usually spat on.

After that, they chose a life of crime. When not in jail, they stole whatever they wanted, and smuggled whatever they could sell. The brothers' latest stint in prison was for hijacking a lorry full of luxury chocolate bars, which would have been delivered to a hospital for poorly orphans if Don, Ron, and Con hadn't taken the chocolate for themselves and crashed the lorry into a ditch.

Now that they were out of prison, they celebrated by robbing the butcher's shop on Craystead High Street, and having a barbecue.

'I agree,' said Don. 'Some people like restaurants, some people prefer takeaways. I say food always tastes better when you've stolen it yourself.' Don seemed relaxed, although it was rarely possible to tell what mood he was in, because he usually glared in a way that could scare off an angry gorilla.

The others nodded. Ron finished his sausage and stood up to get a pork chop from the barbecue, when he heard something rustling in the hedge. 'Look at that!' said Ron, 'There's a little doggy poking his head into our garden. Where did he come from?' Despite a strong dislike of all people except his brothers, Ron liked animals. During one stretch in jail, he looked after chickens on the prison farm.

Scruffy was attracted by the smell of the barbecue, which made him feel even hungrier than he was already. He had now been wandering around Craystead for a couple of days, and it seemed that everywhere he went he could smell the stray dog and the big beef bone that he was searching for. The stray must have dragged that bone down every road in Craystead, and left the scent in all directions. Scruffy was now completely lost, and even messier than usual, after sleeping on someone's flowerbed after a brief thunderstorm the night before. Scruffy had been drinking water out of puddles and drains, and eating whatever he could find in rubbish bins, which was barely enough to feed a hamster.

Ron threw Scruffy a pork chop, and took another for himself. The hungry dog gulped it down in seconds. Then Scruffy ran up to Ron and swiped the second pork chop from the gangster's dirty, cracked plate.

Don and Con chuckled at the look on Ron's face, a blend of surprise and disappointment at losing his snack, with a slight smile of approval mixed in. 'He's just like us,' Ron remarked, 'I reckon I'm going to get on well with this mutt. Maybe there is a fourth member of the Craystead Four after all.'

'He's wearing a collar,' Con observed, with the wonky grin that usually adorned his cruel-looking face, 'so maybe he belongs to someone?'

'Wouldn't bother me,' Don replied.

Ron had a look at the muddy collar. 'He has a name tag, he's called Scruffy. Sounds about right, he's the scruffiest dog I've ever seen. No contact details here. Just a little pocket in his collar, nothing in it.'

'Right, he's one of us now,' Don said, and eased himself out of his garden chair. 'Come here, boy,' he motioned to Scruffy, 'I've got something for you.' Don gave Scruffy a couple of bones, which he'd found among the meat from the butcher's shop. Scruffy wagged his tail in delight.

Don turned to his brothers and announced, 'Lads, I have something for us as well. It's a slide.'

Con tilted his head and asked, 'What, are you building a playground?'

'Not that kind of slide, you plonker,' Don replied, with a shake of his head and a sigh. 'I mean a little photo, you know, the kind that you stick in a projector so you can see it on a screen.'

'What's in this photo?' Ron asked.

'No idea,' Don said, 'I held it up to the light and couldn't see a lot. Must be some kind of code or something. I heard it's a top-secret slide, and there are government people looking for it. Dodgy Dan offered me fifty thousand pounds if I could get it. Then I found out the bloke in the butcher's had it hidden in a drawer under the till, and I pinched it when we robbed the place. We're going to meet Dodgy Dan in Craystead Park this Sunday and hand it over, then we'll be rich.'

'That deserves another sausage!' Ron said, grinning like a monkey with a giant banana, and swaggered back to the barbecue.

Scruffy was still missing his big beef bone, but the stolen bones from the butcher's shop were delicious too, and he was beginning to feel like his old self again. He tried digging a hole to bury one of his new bones so he could save it for later, but the grass hadn't been cut and was thick with weeds, so Scruffy couldn't reach the soil. It just wasn't the same as being at home with Granny.

*   *   *

'I do love a pretty poodle!' said the Queen. 'Who's a good boy?' On her return to Buckingham Palace from her secret bungalow, she decided it would be a brilliant plan to find a stray mongrel to join the royal corgis. A new playmate from the harsh streets, who would be made a prince among dogs. A visit to Craystead Dog Rescue Centre was arranged immediately. The press seemed to enjoy it almost as much as the Queen did, and the photographers followed her around like sheep with cameras, as the manager introduced her to the most well-behaved canines in his care.

The poodle's owner had already been found. The poodle had run away from a dog groomer, who dared to use a cheap shampoo that smelt of mouldy oranges, instead of the luxurious, flower-scented beauty products that the animal was used to. The owners of the fussy pooch contacted the Rescue Centre as soon as the groomer apologized for losing their dog, and they offered a large reward for the return of their priceless pet. The poodle was found that morning, having wandered into an expensive ladies' hairdresser's boutique.

'Never mind,' the Queen said on hearing that this one was not available, 'poodles are wonderful, but not exactly what we're looking for today.' The Queen was joined by two bodyguards and Crackers, her favourite corgi. 'We've also met a dainty dachshund, a beautiful beagle, a delightful Dalmatian, and lots of others like them. All lovely dogs, and I'm sure each one is fit for a queen. Dogs like these must have owners that are missing them, and I would feel awfully guilty taking one of these back to the Palace. I'm looking for a stray, a rough beast — but one that's well-behaved. A dog with a more common touch.' She stepped closer to the manager, and whispered, 'One that readers of *The Sun* would appreciate.'

The manager looked uncomfortable, and replied, 'I understand, ma'am, but I'm not sure we can help. In the other kennels we have a beastly boxer, a menacing mastiff, and even a perilous pit bull. But Your Majesty wouldn't want to meet any of those, and they'd swallow Crackers before Your Majesty can say "cheese". Even a lion tamer would be frightened of some of them.'

'What's really required,' the Queen said, 'is a happy, friendly, messy mongrel.'

'We sometimes have dogs like that here,' the manager answered, 'but they are very popular, and are adopted as soon as anybody meets them. I'll contact the Palace when one comes in.'

The Queen was not too disappointed. It was a pleasant day out for her and Crackers, and the press had taken some good photos. She decided to greet some of the public, and after chatting with several children and their parents, she bumped into three rather untidy boys, who'd just arrived with an old lady.

'Wow, you look just like the Queen!' Sam exclaimed.

'She's not tall enough to be the Queen,' Arnold muttered.

Granny gave Arnold a stern look, and was about to comment on his rudeness, when the Queen laughed and replied, 'I did hear that the Queen was planning to visit Craystead Dog Rescue Centre today.'

Robert chipped in, 'You look just like the lady with a black eye-patch, who lives in the bungalow with the tall privet hedge. She's hardly ever there, though, she must go on a lot of holidays. Are you her sister?'

The Queen stepped back, and narrowed her eyes as if she needed to sneeze. But only for a moment. She chuckled and said, 'I have no idea what you're talking about, and I've never been anywhere near Craystead before. It seems like a marvellous place, especially as there aren't many cats. I am in fact the Queen.'

Robert raised his eyebrows and bit his lip. He didn't feel entirely convinced, but he was far too shy to argue with Her Majesty. The other boys' faces went red like ripe chilli peppers. Granny curtsied and said, 'It's so lovely to meet Your Majesty, and I do apologize for these young chaps. They are helping me find my lost dog. He's nowhere to be found, so we came here to see if he's been rescued.'

The Queen said she was sorry to hear about Granny's missing pet, and asked the dog's name, but before Granny could answer, one of the royal bodyguards pointed at the clock. The Queen had asked him to remind her to leave by four o'clock, so she could return to the Palace in time for a game of snakes and ladders with the Minister of Transport, who didn't like to be kept waiting.

After the Queen left, Arnold and Sam wandered off to tease the dogs and pull silly faces at each other, when a girl approached Robert and Granny. It was Claire from Robert's school, a smiley young lady, with glasses and frizzy hair. 'Did your gran say her dog's gone missing?' she asked.

'Um, yes,' Robert answered, 'and I'm sorry about flicking paper into your hair during that spelling test before. It was funny, though.'

Claire shrugged her shoulders, rolling her head and her eyes. 'If you say so,' she answered. 'I might have seen him. Is he a messy little brown dog, like a Yorkshire terrier but shaped a bit like a cat?'

'That sounds like Scruffy!' Granny chirped. 'Where did you see him?'

Just then, Claire's mother intervened. 'Aren't you Robert, from Claire's school?' she glared. 'I heard about you flicking paper at her. Stop being a bother!'

'I said sorry!' Robert protested.

'Mummy, his gran's lost her dog,' Claire said, 'and his mum and dad were in an accident.'

'I'm so sorry to hear that,' Claire's mother replied, 'are your parents OK?'

'Yes, they're alright,' Robert said, 'they're at a yoga retreat.'

'I love yoga!' Claire's mother exclaimed, 'Especially the Beached Octopus pose.'

'Beached Octopus is a magnificent yoga pose,' Granny commented, 'but enough of that. Claire, where did you see Scruffy?'

'Well,' Claire answered, 'when we were on our way here, I saw a dog like Scruffy scrambling into a hedge. That weird house, where the hedge is all overgrown and some of the windows are broken. There was some smoke, it smelt like a barbecue. Mummy says that house is dangerous, it's been empty for ages but there are some men there now. Mummy says they've just come out of prison.'

'That's right, those three are real troublemakers,' Claire's mother added.

Granny and Robert looked at each other, then called Arnold and Sam over. 'I suppose I'd better go to that house,' Granny said nervously.

'Maybe you should ring the police?' Arnold asked.

'No,' said Granny, 'I don't want to trouble them, and my generation didn't survive a world war without being brave. However nasty those three men are, surely they wouldn't do any harm to a little old lady searching for a lost dog.'

'I'll go with you and watch from my bike,' Sam added, boldly, 'so if something bad happens I can ride to the nearest phone box and call the police.'

'Let me come too, Granny, please,' said Robert, 'I want to see Scruffy again!'

'Fine,' Granny agreed, 'you can come, Robert, but only if you try to look harmless, and don't say anything. I'll have to comb your hair again. Arnold, you'd better go home, your mother worries about you, and I don't want you doing anything disgusting that might start a fight.'

'What could I do that's disgusting?' Arnold asked, while picking his nose and scratching his bottom.

'I shudder to think,' Granny responded. 'Thank you for your help, Claire. Now we'll be on our way and bring Scruffy home!'

Chapter 4

'I do love a real crime!' Sergeant Dobbs announced, as he put the phone down and reached for his half-eaten slice of pizza, topped with chopped Mars bar, anchovies, and plenty of chilli sauce.

'You call yourself a policeman and you love a real crime?' Constable Cloud joked, and flicked an elastic band at his superior.

'I mean, this time we actually have a real crime to deal with, instead of hearing people moan about their missing cats. Now the Three Idiots are out of prison, it was only a matter of time, but I didn't think they'd be daft enough to strike this soon.'

Craystead Police Station was a busy place to work before Don, Ron, and Con went to jail. The brothers used to cause chaos, peddling all kinds of stolen and smuggled goods, daubing graffiti on the houses with the best-kept gardens, and starting fires in dustbins whenever they were bored. Another favourite game of theirs was to rub catnip on sticks, throwing them for dogs that were off their leads in the park, creating awe-inspiring scenes of cat-dog warfare. That was long before cats became a rare sight in Craystead. The police were often called to the parish church, where the brothers liked to detonate stink bombs, but nobody could ever prove who was responsible.

With the brothers in prison, Craystead was peaceful. Now, they were free again.

'Yeah,' replied the constable, 'we've had a lot of people asking about missing cats again lately. Don't know what all the fuss is about. Cats always come home eventually. Anyone would think Craystead is the Bermuda Triangle when it comes to cats. So, the robbery at the butcher's shop was definitely the Three Idiots?'

Don, Ron, and Con had been careful to wear gloves when they carried out their latest crime, but opening the draw under the till was awkward, so Don removed his gloves when he stole the top-secret slide. Forensics had found a fingerprint. A flange of baboons would have made a better job of covering their tracks at a robbery, and funnily enough, Don, Ron, and Con had been wearing baboon masks at the time.

'That's right,' said the sergeant, 'we can't use the cells for yoga practice this evening, we have some arrests to make.'

'No way!' the constable replied, 'I was hoping to have a go at Beached Octopus tonight. That's a magnificent yoga pose.'

Sergeant Dobbs and Constable Cloud called for more policemen to accompany them, and headed straight for the brothers' house. A colleague would join them to arrest the three brothers, and another three officers would wait in a car outside, in case help would be needed. What could possibly go wrong?

*   *   *

'He really loves his bones!' Con said, pointing at Scruffy and Ron. The pair were engaged in a tug-of-war. Scruffy growled and balanced awkwardly on his hind legs while Ron teased him, yanking on the bone in his mouth. Ron pulled to one side, then to another, then dragged Scruffy all the way round in a circle. The snarling dog would not let go, even though all of his feet were off the ground a couple of times.

'He'll come in really useful for any jobs involving bones,' said Don.

'Hey, I've got an idea!' Con exclaimed, 'We could go all over Surrey robbing butchers' shops. Scruffy will be our secret weapon.'

'That's a thought,' Don replied. 'We could take Scruffy with us on each job. He'd go crazy in any butcher's shop. When the staff are trying to protect their precious meat, we'll put sacks over their heads and tie them up. Then we'll take everything we can and empty the tills.'

'And we'll give Scruffy lots of bones, that'll be his share of the loot,' Ron added, as he let Scruffy go. Scruffy scampered into a corner, where he gleefully sucked and nibbled on his bone. 'Here,' said Ron, 'let's have a look at this amazing slide of yours, Don, the one that'll earn us fifty thousand pounds.'

Don shiftily looked around to check there were no prying eyes in any neighbouring windows, then reached for his wallet and took out the slide, handing it to Ron. 'Careful with it,' he muttered with his usual stern scowl.

Ron held the slide up to the sunlight. 'You're right, can't really see any kind of picture, no colours. The cardboard mount around the edge has some sort of logo. It looks like a royal coat of arms or something.'

'I said the government's looking for it. Perhaps it's a document?' Don pondered.

'Hey, it could be a treasure map!' Con interjected. 'Maybe there's some secret government vault with loads of gold bars or piles of money hidden inside. That would explain why Dodgy Dan's happy to pay so much for it.'

'If it's a map, it must be really detailed,' Ron said, 'I can't see any shapes or anything.'

'Good point, Con,' said Don. 'Let's get a slide projector and have a proper look at it. I asked Dodgy Dan what's on this slide, and he acted like he didn't know. I thought it was a rare antique picture or something, but it clearly isn't that. If it's a clue about a bigger prize, we have to find out so we can get it.'

Just at that moment, they heard a loud knocking on the front door. Scruffy leapt to the middle of the garden and began running in circles, barking as if a dozen squirrels had bitten his tail.

'Come here, boy,' Ron said softly, 'It's probably just another old lady looking for a lost cat. Already had one of those this morning. Let's ignore it.' Scruffy calmed down and rolled on the grass next to Ron.

'What's happening with all the cats?' Con pondered. 'There always used to be loads of them in Craystead. Haven't seen any since we got back here, but there are posters about lost cats all over the place.'

There was more knocking on the door, and some shouting: 'Police, open up!'

'It's the peelers,' said Don. 'Quick Ron, hide the slide while I get the car keys!'

'Where shall I hide it?'

'Anywhere, just not in your clothes. If they arrest us, they'll search us,' Don answered, as he nipped through the back door.

Ron thought for a moment, then remembered the little pocket in Scruffy's collar. Was it big enough for the slide? Ron slipped it in there, and it was a perfect fit.

'Good afternoon, Constable Dobbs, it's a pleasure to see you again!' Don said as he stepped back into the garden. Three policemen had entered through the gate, bearing their truncheons like knights going into battle. Don was forcing a smile, the rest of his face screwed up in his usual angry grimace.

'It's sergeant now,' Dobbs answered.

'Congratulations on your promotion,' Don responded, 'would you like to join us at our barbecue to celebrate?'

'Those sausages look jolly tasty!' Constable Cloud remarked.

'We'll grab some sausages on our way out,' Dobbs said. 'We're here to take you lot to the police station for a chat about the butcher's shop on the High Street.' Turning to Cloud, he added, 'You'd better not eat the evidence.'

'Sergeant, sergeant,' Don said, 'there's no evidence here. We haven't done anything. Have a close look at this bone. You can't get bones like this in Craystead High Street.' He picked up Scruffy's bone from the grass, and handed it to Dobbs, who raised an eyebrow and examined it, looking puzzled. 'Scruffy!' Don yelled. 'He's got your bone!'

Scruffy leapt into the air, and for a few seconds his little legs whizzed like a tornado of feet, and he barked so loudly that the brothers and two of the policemen gasped and went pale. Scruffy paused and wheezed, already out of breath from the excitement. Then he pounced on Sergeant Dobbs, who held up his hands, releasing the bone and dropping his truncheon. 'Call for backup!' he shouted at Constable Cloud.

Cloud was the one policeman that didn't panic at Scruffy's rage. He had a soft spot for dogs. 'We don't need backup,' he answered confidently. 'He's just a lovely little doggy! Here boy, what a nice treat you have there, does it taste good? Tasty bone for a special doggy?'

The third policeman yelled, 'Back up needed now!' into his walkie talkie, and hastily bent down to find Dobbs's truncheon, which had landed in a particularly overgrown patch of weeds. Dobbs stared at Cloud and Scruffy in bewilderment.

With the policemen distracted, Don, Ron, and Con chose this moment to sneak into the back door, quietly and swiftly, then escape out of the front. The police cars there were empty, and three more policemen could be seen rushing down the alleyway at the side of the house.

The brothers breathed sighs of relief, as Don unlocked his car door and climbed into the driver's seat. 'A smooth getaway for the Craystead Four!' he announced, as he let his brothers in.

Con caught his sleeve on the car door handle. As he hurriedly fiddled with it, an old lady in a colourful cardigan approached him. 'Excuse me, sir,' Granny said sweetly, 'my grandson and I are looking for a dog. We heard he might be here, have you seen him?' Robert stood anxiously behind his grandmother, hiding his face, but held her hand to give her support, as he knew she was nervous too.

'We're in a bit of a rush,' Con answered, as he freed his sleeve, 'but there is a dog in the back garden, might be yours, go down the alley and have a look. Gate's open.'

Ron stared at Con in disbelief, with a look of horror as he remembered where the slide was hidden.

'Thank you so much, dear, you're awfully kind,' Granny smiled.

Con jumped into his seat, and Don drove his brothers away faster than a rat pursued by a hungry fox.

'What did you tell her that for?' Ron protested, 'I hid the slide in his collar!'

'It makes a change from lost cats,' Con replied.

'Don't worry,' Don said calmly, 'I recognize her, she lives just around the corner. We'll go there later and say we're checking Scruffy's alright. Then we can get the slide.'

The policemen in the garden heard the screech of the car speeding off, and knew they'd failed. Sergeant Dobbs put his hands in his pockets and frowned. Cloud scratched his head, looked at Dobbs, glanced at Scruffy, then at Dobbs again, and shrugged.

Scruffy growled, wagged his tail, and stared at the back gate. The policemen followed his gaze, to see another dog standing there, with a bone much thicker and more impressive than the one Scruffy had in front of him. It was the same stray that took Scruffy's favourite bone from Granny's garden days earlier, and the stray was holding that same succulent beef bone in his mouth! Noticing Scruffy, he ran away, and Scruffy took off in pursuit, in a cacophony of barks.

'Right,' Constable Cloud said, 'does that mean I can have a sausage now?'

'Just one won't do any harm, I suppose,' Dobbs answered.

Moments later, Granny and Robert appeared at the gate, with expectant faces. 'Excuse me, have any of you gentlemen seen a little dog?' Granny asked, 'I heard barking.'

'Are you looking for a messy little dog, brown, about the same size as a cat?' Dobbs asked.

'That matches his description exactly!' Granny replied. 'He's been missing since Tuesday.'

'We're really looking forward to seeing him again,' Robert added.

'I'm sorry, but you've just missed him,' said the sergeant, 'he saw another dog and scarpered. No idea where he's gone, I've never seen a dog run so fast. Give me your name and telephone number. We'll be in touch if one of us sees him.'

The policemen went inside the house to search for baboon masks, gloves, and any other evidence linking the brothers to the robbery. Granny and Robert were left standing in the garden, and Sam arrived on his bicycle to join them.

'Did you find Scruffy?' Sam asked.

'No, but we were so close!' Robert answered, the frustration obvious in his voice.

Granny looked distraught, and she wiped her eyes with a tissue from her handbag. 'They said he was here a moment ago! It's like we're doomed to never see him again. We've looked everywhere and tried everything.'

'I didn't see him from the front when I was watching from my bike, just heard some barking,' Sam replied, 'so he must have gone in the other direction down the alley. Shall I go and ride around looking for him?'

'Thanks,' said Granny, 'that's a nice idea. I need a rest and I'm taking Robert home, but I really hope you find him.' Granny sighed, and Robert kept looking at his feet. The pair were beginning to lose hope, but Sam was becoming more determined.

Chapter 5

'I do love winning!' the Prime Minister exclaimed, rubbing his hands together. That morning he had joined the Queen for snakes and ladders. She won the first two games, but went on to lose the next three. So, it was time for a forfeit. The Prime Minister ordered the Queen to sing and dance the Hokey Cokey with the milk jug from her favourite tea set balanced on top of her head.

The Queen made an impressive job of the task to begin with, putting her right arm in and her right arm out several times, with the jug hardly wobbling at all. But every time the Queen dances the Hokey Cokey, her favourite part is shaking it all about, which she does with a lot of energy. Sure enough, at that moment the small jug went flying straight at the Prime Minister, who caught it skilfully with one hand, but not without milk spilling everywhere.

The Prime Minister giggled like a cartoon monkey, while he wiped splattered milk from his spectacles. The Queen looked at the soaked sleeve of her dress, and made a face like a bulldog swallowing a cricket ball. Calling on a servant to clean the room, the Queen explained, 'I'm ever so sorry. We were just discussing the economy, and I dropped the milk.'

'Of course, ma'am,' the servant replied. 'Would Your Majesty like me to put the snakes and ladders away too?'

The Queen's face went the same colour as the flesh of a water melon, which was interesting because her dress was the colour of a water melon's skin. 'Oh yes, thank you. We weren't actually playing snakes and ladders, of course,' the Queen chuckled nervously, 'Mr Major was merely using the game to show me how the economy works. It goes up like the ladders, and down like the snakes. Mostly snakes at the moment.'

This was not a good start to the day, so the Queen decided to make the afternoon better. She resolved that this was going to be the day she'd find a stray dog to join her pack of corgis, and when the Queen resolves to do something, she usually achieves it.

Once the mess was cleaned up and she had changed her clothes, the Queen called a chauffeur and a bodyguard to take her and Crackers to Craystead and drive around. It was just beginning to rain, and there were some rumbles of thunder, when she noticed something unusual about one house.

'Look at that, driver,' said the Queen, 'there are two cats in that window, and one of them seems rather familiar. There's an unusual mark on his forehead, which I'm sure I've seen before. Stop the car while I think.'

The chauffeur parked in front of the house, and the Queen pondered for a few seconds. Then she announced, 'That's a cat that went missing! I saw his photo on a poster.'

'Where did Your Majesty see the poster?' the driver asked.

'Never mind that,' answered the Queen, handing her corgi a biscuit. 'Give me an umbrella, wait here, and keep an eye on Crackers. I'm going to investigate.'

*   *   *

'I do love a juicy bogey!' Arnold announced, gleefully extracting a large green globule from his nose and plonking it into his mouth. Mrs Pittick glanced up from weeding the flowerbed, and mumbled a response that sounded rude. 'You are always telling me to eat my greens,' Arnold muttered.

Sam arrived on his bicycle with a loud brrrppp of his brakes.

'Hi Sam, is Scruffy back at home now?' Arnold asked.

'No, he isn't,' Sam replied, 'Let me leave my bike here and we'll go and meet Robert. I'll tell you all about what happened yesterday while we're on the way.'

'Take your jacket!' Mrs Pittick told her son, 'I know it's sunny now but it might be wet later.'

When they arrived at Granny's house, Robert answered the door. 'Granny seems really fed up today and she says she won't go out,' Robert said. 'I think she's losing hope of ever finding Scruffy. Maybe I should stay here and keep her company.'

'Rubbish!' Sam retorted, 'Just think how happy she'll be when we bring him home. Today's the day we're going to find Scruffy!'

Two hours later, it was starting to rain, and Robert, Arnold, and Sam stood in a bus shelter on Craystead High Street. They had been feeling confident earlier, but now appeared forlorn.

'We've searched everywhere,' Arnold said.

'There are still places we could look!' Sam replied, trying to seem optimistic.

'Where, oh where, oh where is Scruffy?' Robert yelped in frustration, shaking his head and furiously fiddling with the zip on his jacket.

Suddenly, three big ugly men stood in front of them, blocking any means of escape. With a fearsome grimace, and a booming voice, one of them asked, 'Did you say Scruffy?'

'Hey, I know you from somewhere!' Sam said. Then he recognized Don as one of the men he saw the day before, and interrupted himself. 'Errrmmm, no, actually I don't know you, sorry.'

So far, it had been an eventful day for Don, Ron, and Con. Right after Robert went out with his friends, Don knocked on Granny's door to ask whether Scruffy was OK, and he planned to recover the top-secret slide.

In the brothers' annoyance at Scruffy's absence, they went to the grocer's shop on the High Street and shoplifted three bananas. They were slightly reluctant to enter that shop, because the sight of cauliflowers and sprouts always brought back bad memories from their schooldays, but they had a purpose for the bananas. From there they went to the sweet shop, where they held the bananas under their T-shirts to pretend that they had guns, and ordered the man behind the counter to give them bags of all their favourite treats.

Leaving the sweet shop, they headed to the bus shelter to stand out of the rain, while talking about how to track down Scruffy. That's when they overheard the three boys discussing the same topic.

'We have lots of sweets,' Con said with his wonky smile, 'why don't you boys come with us, and we can have a chat about Scruffy?'

Robert started shaking. He knew he must never talk to strangers, especially if they offer sweets. Arnold looked at his shoes and moaned. Sam glanced at his friends, raised his chin, and admitted, 'I don't think we have much choice.'

The car was parked close by, and soon the boys were crammed tightly into the back seats, with Ron and Con either side of them. Robert, Sam, and Arnold were squashed up together so uncomfortably that it was difficult to breathe, which added to their anxiety. Don drove them to the brother's hideout. Every tree and lamppost seemed to be twisted into a threatening shape by the rainwater trickling down the windows.

The hideout was the dirtiest place the boys had ever seen. Arnold, fascinated by all things disgusting, gazed around himself in awe, wondering how anywhere could be so filthy. Sam was determined not to show any fear, but Robert couldn't hide his trembling lips. Robert sneezed on the way in, and his eyes went pink, from the dust and from the feathers that were stuck to the floor and the walls. The hideout was a small flat, which had recently been used to keep racing pigeons. There were three uncomfortable-looking metal chairs in the middle of the room, and behind the chairs stood some empty wire cages with high wooden backs. It was dark, but a flash of lightning revealed that everything was covered in bird droppings. A rumble of thunder echoed around the room, and a subtle smell of mould wafted through the air.

'Tie them up and we'll get started,' Don said to his brothers, and a few minutes later Robert, Arnold, and Sam were bound to the chairs by their ankles and waists, their hands tied behind their backs.

'What do we do now?' Ron asked.

Don raised his eyebrows, looked to one side, and answered, 'Well, we have to make them tell us everything they know about Scruffy.'

'How do we do that, then?' Ron replied.

Con turned to the boys, with his best attempt at a friendly smile, and said, 'Right, lads, if you tell me everything you know about Scruffy, I'll give you some sweeties!'

Robert and Arnold stayed quiet, their eyes pointing at their knees, but Sam chose to be bold. 'There's nothing to tell,' he said, 'Scruffy's a dog, he's gone missing, and we're looking for him, that's it.'

Ron gestured to Don and Con to come closer to him, and he whispered, 'Maybe we're being stupid. These kids don't know any more than we do. Why are we bothering with all this?'

'These boys know about Scruffy,' Don replied firmly. 'If they know where Scruffy is, we have to make them tell us. If not, maybe they'll give us some clues. Do you have any better ideas?'

'We could make them do yoga,' Con suggested, 'that's my idea of torture.'

Ron added, 'Hey, do you remember when they tried to make us do a yoga class in jail?'

'Remember it?' Con answered, 'Of course I remember it, that was the best time I ever had in prison! We started a riot, and the yoga instructor had to go to hospital afterwards. That's what you get for trying to make the Craystead Four do the Beached Octopus pose.'

'Beached Octopus is a magnificent yoga pose!' said Don, 'But we can't get them to do yoga, we've tied them up. I have a much better idea.' Don plucked a feather from the grubby floor. 'This will make them talk. Take off their shoes and socks.'

Don approached Robert first, tickling the soles of his feet for a full minute. Robert howled and spluttered with laughter, until his eyes were dripping with tears.

'Now,' said Don, 'you tell me where Scruffy is, or I'll do that again, it'll be two minutes next time.'

'I don't know where he is!' Robert protested, 'I'm looking for him. He's my granny's dog. We've searched all over the place. I saw you three yesterday, you were getting into a car outside your house. Granny asked about Scruffy and he was in your garden, I was standing behind her. But Scruffy was gone. That's all I know!'

'That sounds about right,' said Con, but Don was too paranoid to accept Robert's answer. A flicker of lightning made Don's glaring features even more ominous.

'You're lying. You heard about that from someone else, now you're pretending you were there. I don't remember seeing some little red-haired kid outside our house,' Don insisted. 'You're next,' he added, scowling at Sam.

'I'm not ticklish!' Sam grinned. Don tickled Sam's toes, lifted his T-shirt and tickled his tummy, and even tried tickling his neck, but Sam stayed still and quiet and proudly watched as Don became more and more frustrated.

'Right, it's your turn,' Don growled at Arnold, like a tiger ready to pounce on a rabbit.

'No, leave me alone. I hate being tickled!' Arnold yelled. 'I'm not going to let you tickle me!'

Don responded, 'How are you going to stop me?'

Arnold pouted, and wrinkled his forehead. His face began to change colour, first pink, then red, then purple. His cheeks began to swell, and he pressed his elbows into his sides, while clenching his fists so hard that his knuckles went white and knobbly.

'You don't want to go near him now,' Sam warned. 'I'd step back if I were you.' Sam knew what was coming. He'd witnessed this once before, when a dinner lady told Arnold to eat all of his liver and onions before he could have any pudding.

Don ignored Sam's advice, and bent down in front of Arnold, reaching towards the boy's left foot with the feather.

The room was immediately flooded with a loud roar. It was like the sound of an old motorcycle racing at full speed through a tunnel, much louder than any of the rolls of thunder that could be heard from outside. Arnold's incredible fart was so deafening that Don held his ears and shrieked, but he should have covered his nose instead. Within moments, the sickening stench of Arnold's fart hit Don in the face like a heavyweight boxer with a concrete fist.

Don stood up awkwardly, wobbling from side to side, with his eyes streaming. After choking a few times, Don croaked at his brothers, 'Get out of here before the smell gets to you.'

Ron and Con didn't need to be told, and were already scuttling to the door, gripping their noses. Don followed, shut the door, and the boys were left alone.

'Oh, that stinks, Arnold,' Sam moaned, his eyes now watering too.

'Of course it stinks, I had my favourite breakfast this morning: beans and rhubarb. It got rid of them, so don't complain,' Arnold replied. 'You remember that trick I can do with my hands? When they tied us up, they didn't know I'm double jointed.' With that, Arnold jiggled his shoulders, twisted his arms over his head, and used his teeth to unravel the knot that held his wrists together. 'I've tried that before!' he said triumphantly, reaching down to untie the other ropes that held him in the chair, then released his friends from their bonds.

'That's amazing, Arnold,' Robert declared.

'Yes, it is,' Sam agreed, 'but let's be quiet, they might be right outside that door, and could come back any second. Let's hide behind those cages, and keep hold of the ropes. I have a plan.'

The door handle turned with a creak, and Ron scurried across the room to open the window, still holding his nose. Then he sprayed some air freshener. Noticing the chairs were empty, he shouted to Don and Con, 'Hey, they've gone!'

'They've left their shoes and socks behind,' Don observed, as he entered and sat down.

'Did they go out of the window?' Con asked.

'Must have done, I suppose,' Ron answered, 'but the window was shut when I came back in.'

Ron and Con sat down with Don.

'That was a waste of time,' Ron said. The brothers nodded and stared at the walls, listening to the rain and the thunder, which were now getting quieter.

Robert, Sam, and Arnold silently tiptoed out from behind the cages, holding up the ropes, with loose knots already prepared. A moment later they were standing behind the Craystead Four, who hadn't noticed the boys. Holding up the ropes, Robert and Arnold glanced at Sam, who nodded. That was the signal, and the three boys immediately thrust the ropes down over the brothers' heads and around their waists, and pulled the knots tight to trap the men in their chairs. With cries of shock, Don, Ron, and Con stood up, but the chairs were clunky and awkward and they immediately toppled over.

'Now it's time for revenge!' Robert proclaimed, picking up a feather, with confidence that was unusual for him.

'Don't bother, Robert,' Sam said, 'there's no point, and they'll undo those ropes in no time. Let's just go.'

Robert didn't listen to Sam, and Arnold joined Robert in removing the three brothers' shoes and socks.

'Remember what you did?' Con said, staring angrily at Arnold. 'I can do better!' Con twisted his face, closing one eye while the other eye bulged, and his cheeks went crimson. Then he squirmed like a slug, and gasped. But all Con could manage was a small squeak, like a mouse caught in a box. His fart was nothing compared to Arnold's gas monster.

Robert, Sam, and Arnold sniggered, put their shoes on, and walked through the door, down the stairs, and into the street, where there were some enormous puddles. The storm had ended, sunshine was creeping through the clouds, and a rainbow shimmered in the distance.

'It's been raining cats and dogs,' Arnold said.

'Just cats,' Sam replied, 'look at that!' Sam pointed at three rather damp cats sauntering across the road.

'Wow,' Robert added, 'I haven't seen any cats around here for ages. Maybe all the missing cats are coming home. If that can happen, Scruffy can come home too! I wonder where they came from?'

Chapter 6

'I do love a house with lots of cats,' said the Queen, with one of her friendliest smiles, 'and those are some particularly pretty pussies in your window.'

'Window?' came a squawked reply. 'Are you trying to sell me double glazing? I don't want it and neither do my cats.'

The Queen peered around the edge of the front door, which was open just a few inches. The lady staring back at her from the shadowy interior had long, wild, grey hair and scratches on her face. It was difficult to tell whether the lady was wearing a cardigan or a dressing gown, but whatever it was, it was covered with dust and small hairs.

'I certainly don't want to talk about double glazing,' the Queen replied firmly. 'I am the Queen. I am merely visiting the area, and thought it would be nice to meet some of my subjects. Today I am accompanied by Barry, my best bodyguard.'

'I'll believe it when I see it!' the wild-haired lady screeched. 'Hang on, I'll go and get my glasses. Not sure where I left them, I hate wearing those things.'

The door slammed and the Queen glanced around. The cats in the window jumped out of sight, then three others came into view. 'Those ones look familiar as well,' the Queen murmured to Barry, 'I think I've seen those on lost cat posters too. Let's see what's going on here, then get back to looking for a stray dog.'

The house looked tired and dreary, with paint peeling off the door frame, three rusty watering cans next to the doorstep, and an untidy assortment of weeds sprouting through the cracks in the poorly tarmacked driveway. The rain became harder and a bolt of lightning could be seen nearby. The door opened again.

'Ods bodkins! It really is the Queen! Come in, Your Majesty, and say hello to all my cats. I have some playful Persians, some boisterous Bengals, and some refulgent ragdolls. My name's Doris. Come this way, you can sit in my lounge.'

The Queen twitched slightly. She didn't want to admit that she didn't know what 'refulgent' means. After being ushered in, she noticed that the dirty settee and armchairs were occupied by dozens of felines, some of whom were sleeping, others scratching and licking themselves. Hundreds more were crowded around the room. 'I'd prefer to stand,' the Queen said.

'Jolly good, can I get you and your friend a cup of tea?' Doris asked, trying to curtsy but nearly tripping over a Russian blue that was clawing at her mucky slippers.

'Yes please,' the Queen replied, 'just a drop of milk and no sugar, thank you.'

Doris pushed her way through a swarm of cats vying for her attention — it seemed the animals were hungry — and when the Queen heard the sound of a kettle being filled, she turned to her bodyguard and asked, 'What does "refulgent" mean?'

'It means brilliant, ma'am,' Barry answered.

'Correct,' she replied. 'Just testing!' Then she whispered, 'This lady is possibly quite mad. Let's be kind to her, but we have to get these creatures out of here. Cats have been disappearing all over Craystead for some time. She clearly cannot help herself from collecting them and imprisoning them right here.'

'Does Your Majesty have a plan?' Barry answered, in a hushed voice. 'Cats hate going out in the rain, and there's a storm going on.' At that moment, there was a bright flash and a deep roll of thunder, and the rain on the window grew even louder.

'This is the perfect time to do it,' the Queen replied. 'If we set them free now, they will go straight back to their homes!'

Doris emerged from the kitchen with two mugs, which were decorated with pictures of Bagpuss. A large tabby jumped off the dining table and on to Doris's face, and she dropped the cups of tea, waving her arms like a windmill in a whirlpool. After clumsily removing the animal, she bent down to find her spectacles, and put them in her pocket. 'Zooterkins!' she shrieked, 'Sorry, Your Majesty, I'll put the kettle on again.'

Once Doris was back in the kitchen, the Queen told Barry, 'I have an idea. I'll follow her in there and keep her busy. Go and get those watering cans from outside, find the bathroom and fill them with water, then leave them in the hallway and meet us in the kitchen. Keep hold of the umbrella.'

The Queen waded through the sprawling mass of felines and joined Doris, who was squinting into a tin containing a mixture of teabags, cat treats, and dead mice.

'Your cats are all really lovely,' said the Queen, before realizing that she didn't have much to talk to Doris about. The Queen has had a strong dislike for cats ever since one crept into her secret bungalow and stole a slice of pizza while she was falling asleep during *Coronation*

Street. She bit her tongue for a few seconds, struggling to think of something Doris would find amusing, then asked the first question that came into her head. 'Do you ever do yoga?'

'I used to do a lot of yoga in the swinging sixties,' Doris answered, 'and my favourite pose was the Beached Octopus.'

'Fascinating,' the Queen replied, doing her best to sound interested, 'Beached Octopus is a magnificent yoga pose!'

Barry arrived, with a small Siamese perched on his shoulder. 'I'm back, ma'am,' he announced. 'Sorry, Doris, I just had to use your loo.'

'Ah, Barry, I'm glad you're back,' said the Queen. 'Doris was just telling me she'd like to show you her garden.'

'Was I?' Doris responded. 'But it's raining?'

'You should get a conservatory!' Barry answered.

'Are you sure you're not trying to sell me double glazing?' Doris said.

'Don't be silly!' the Queen retorted. 'Double glazing is so ugly. Do you think I'd want it in Windsor Castle? Barry loves gardens and he'd like to see yours, and he particularly loves the rain so now's the best time. He's carrying an umbrella especially.'

Once Barry and Doris had stepped into the back garden, which looked more like a jungle, the Queen went to the front door, closing the living room door behind her, and took a can opener and two large tins of pilchards out of her handbag. If you've ever wondered what the Queen keeps in her handbag, now you know. She feels pilchards are the perfect snack whenever she gets peckish during her royal duties. Opening both tins, she made a trail of pilchards outside, leading from the doorstep to the pavement. Luckily the rain was now becoming less heavy.

The Queen went back inside, and opened the living room door. Smelling the pilchards, the hungriest cats ran straight out, but many of the cats were asleep, and most of them were unwilling to go into the rain. The Queen was surprised that so few cats were interested in the pilchards, but she's never had much understanding of feline behaviour, and is much more comfortable with dogs.

So, the Queen picked up a watering can, and started sprinkling its contents all over the poor animals. They hated the water. Some of them arched their backs in shock, and there were a lot of loud miaows and hisses. Many of them ran outside, but there were still at least a hundred cats in the living room when the watering can was empty.

Doris could be heard entering the kitchen through the back door. 'I must see what all that noise is about!' she squawked.

'Don't worry, Her Majesty is probably playing some fun games with your pets,' Barry protested. 'She simply adores cats.' The Queen shuddered and winced at that remark. Barry added, 'Show me more of those stinging nettles. They're gorgeous in this weather.'

Doris grumbled a muffled response, and the Queen sighed with relief as she listened to them returning to the garden.

Knowing she had to act fast, the Queen took the two watering cans that were still full, and spun around in circles, giving all the remaining cats a thorough soaking. The thunderstorm was nothing in comparison to this deluge, and the animals promptly rushed out of the house.

Now feeling rather dizzy, the Queen examined the scene outside. The driveway was covered in cats, climbing over each other in excitement at the smell of the pilchards, although by then all the fish must have been eaten. Some of the felines were already wandering up the road. 'Soon, they'll all go home,' the Queen said to herself with a satisfied grin, and shut the door so they couldn't re-enter. The cats started making a lot of noise, and the Queen thought she could hear a dog barking in the commotion. The sounds went quiet as the cats dispersed.

Doris and Barry returned a few minutes later. 'Those were some beautiful thistles,' Barry said.

'Lawks a mussy! Where are all my cats?' screamed Doris.

'I've let them all go,' the Queen announced. 'I'm awfully sorry, but I know what you've been up to. They weren't your pets and it's about time they went back to their families.'

Doris's eyes were filled with tears, and her face was a bundle of emotions.

'I know you'll miss them,' the Queen said. 'However, it was the right thing to do. I shall arrange counselling for you, and send you a kitten to be your friend.'

Doris replied, 'Every cloud has a silver lining, I suppose.' Despite her tears, she already seemed relieved. Caring for so many cats had become a challenge.

The Queen left the house, and the rain turned into light drizzle. To her surprise, a small dog ran up to her, wagged his tail, and barked. It was Scruffy! 'You're perfect!' the Queen cried in amazement at the sight of the bedraggled mongrel. When she picked him up, Scruffy reacted in the same way as when he had met Doris several days earlier, going completely silent, still, and shaking a little. 'And so well behaved!' the Queen continued, 'Never before have I met a dog that goes so quiet when I hold him. I'm taking you to my special bungalow, where you can get dry.'

'Has Your Majesty made a new friend?' the chauffeur asked as he stepped out of the waiting car.

'Yes, he's wonderful!' the Queen answered with glee. 'Give him a biscuit, and hand me a lead, I'm going to take him and Crackers for a walk together. He's called Scruffy, there's a nametag on his collar. Such a shame there's no phone number on there. I'll just have to keep him! Barry, give me your raincoat and get back in the car, you may return to the Palace.'

'Won't Your Majesty need a bodyguard if Your Majesty is going for a walk?' Barry asked.

The Queen put on the raincoat, which was several sizes too large. 'Nobody will recognize me dressed like this,' she answered, as she took a black eye-patch out of her handbag, slipped a lead on to Scruffy's collar, and took Crackers' lead in her left hand. Crackers and Scruffy stared at each other and growled softly.

*   *   *

Scruffy had an awful time before he met the Queen. After running from the Craystead Four, he followed the stray that had his favourite bone, and this time Scruffy didn't get lost, despite plunging into a pond when distracted by a frog that jumped on to his back. Fortunately for Scruffy, the stray was distracted too, by some ducks waddling briskly away from the pond after Scruffy's accidental dive, so Scruffy didn't lose sight or scent of the dog he was pursuing.

The stray turned out to be the leader of a pack of stray dogs, who had a cosy den in a disused shed in Craystead Park. At first, they welcomed Scruffy, and let him eat some leftovers they'd stolen from a nearby burger van. He had a pleasant night's sleep in the old shed, but the next morning Scruffy was banished from the group, after grappling with the top dog for ownership of Scruffy's beloved beef bone.

Scruffy then spent a few hours joyfully bothering squirrels in the park, until an unusually large squirrel launched himself at Scruffy and scared the dog away, and Scruffy ran through the streets until he found a quiet place for a nap, under some brambles in an alleyway, which sheltered him from the rain. This was right next to Doris's house, and when the hundreds of cats were released,

Scruffy went wild, running in circles and making as much noise as he could, until all the cats had scattered.

The sun came out when Scruffy arrived at the secret bungalow with the Queen and Crackers, and Scruffy seemed to like his new surroundings, which smelled a little bit like Granny's house.

The Queen gave Scruffy a biscuit, and he took it straight to Crackers' bed. Crackers reacted with snarls, and when Scruffy froze in fright Crackers became even more annoyed, bursting into a frenzy of ferocious barking. 'Play nicely with your adorable new friend!' the Queen protested, but Crackers would not stop, so the Queen banished her angry corgi to the garden, where Crackers curled up and sulked under the trampoline.

'One is so happy to have met you, Scruffy!' The Queen announced. 'One shall do some baking to celebrate, and then we shall watch *Neighbours* together. After that, time for pizza!'

Scruffy fell asleep, and the Queen wondered what to bake. To get ideas she took a box out of the sideboard, set up a slide projector, and closed the curtains. The box had 'Princess Marina' written on the side. Princess Marina was a much-loved member of the Royal Family until she passed away in 1968, and she used to compete with the Queen Mother to see who could do the best impressions of various politicians and comedy characters from the wireless. Baking was the princess's passion. As she was very secretive about her recipes, she had them put on to photographic slides instead of writing them down on paper. The Queen placed a handful of slides into the projector, and flicked through the recipes.

The first one described how to make a sausage roll with snails instead of sausages. The Queen was not impressed, especially as the shells would be left on the snails to make the snack extra crunchy. Another recipe was for courgettes stuffed with chocolate and wrapped in bacon. The Queen liked the sound of that. Then the Queen saw Princess Marina's recipe for fruit scones, which included golden syrup and treacle to make them really, really sweet. The Queen was pleased by this, because it reminded her of her own recipe for scones, which she once typed up as a gift for President Eisenhower in 1959.

The Queen chose to make the fruit scones, because they would be her first scones for many years. Last time she made scones that sweet was when Prince Charles was a boy. The sugar gave him so much energy that he jumped up and down until his head hit the ceiling, but then a he got a terrible headache and had to go to bed, so the Queen stopped making them.

The Queen mixed the ingredients, and as she popped the treats into the oven to bake, she remembered that one slide was missing from the collection: Princess Marina's recipe for cheese scones, which had got lost sometime in the 1970s. The Queen and her servants had looked all over Buckingham Palace, and MI5 had searched all over the country, but nobody ever found the lost slide, and the Queen had given up hope of ever attempting Princess Marina's cheese scone recipe.

Before the Queen could get sentimental, Scruffy rushed into the kitchen, jumped on to the table, and knocked over a big bag of flour. The white powder filled the air and coated half the room like a fresh fall of snow. The Queen looked like a ghost, and Scruffy looked like a tiny polar bear, so she put him out in the garden so she could clean up before watching *Neighbours*.

Scruffy meandered across the grass, sniffing the ground, then started squeezing a squeaky toy that belonged to Crackers. The cranky corgi barked and bounded up to Scruffy, and the pair wrestled in a cloud of flour until Crackers snatched the toy and scuttled under the trampoline, watching Scruffy until he settled down in a shady spot several yards away.

'They don't seem to be getting on very well so far,' the Queen thought, as she picked up the dustpan and brush. 'Let's hope one's other corgis like Scruffy. He'll be meeting them tomorrow!'

Chapter 7

'I do love a film about dinosaurs,' said Granny, 'but that one was too scary for me.' She had just taken Robert to the cinema, to take their minds off Scruffy, but it neither lightened their mood nor stopped them worrying.

'It wasn't scary, it was cool,' Robert answered. 'Do you remember when the man was on the toilet and the T-rex ate him?'

'Yes, I do,' Granny replied, 'and I'm amazed boys your age are allowed to watch films with toilets and things. When your mum and dad get back, don't tell them I let you see it. In my young days it was just cartoon rabbits and funny dogs.' Mentioning dogs made them both feel sad. Robert sighed and Granny wiped her eyes. 'Poor Scruffy,' she groaned, 'he disappeared on Tuesday and now it's Saturday. He could be crawling in a ditch somewhere like that fat man in the film.'

'Maybe I should go out and look for him again?' Robert asked.

'Not after what happened to you and your friends yesterday with those awful men,' Granny said, shaking her head. 'Maybe we'll just have to pick out a photo, make a poster, and do some photocopies in the library on Monday.'

'We can't give up after only a few days,' Robert moaned.

'I'm not giving up. I just don't know what to do.'

Granny switched on the television, and Robert was disappointed to see people discussing golf, which he felt was the most boring sport in the world. 'Do you remember when we took Scruffy for a walk near a golf course?' Granny asked.

'That was brilliant,' said Robert. 'That ball landed near him and he picked it up and ran around with it, then that man in silly trousers shouted at him and threatened to do something gross with his putter. I can't believe anyone takes golf so seriously.'

'Yes, and then Scruffy ran up to him, dropped the ball at his feet, and wagged his tail like he was playing fetch,' Granny chuckled, with sadness in her voice. 'Maybe it would have been alright if a seagull hadn't swooped down and swallowed the ball right at that moment! I felt quite sorry for the seagull after what that man did next.'

Robert opened a box of toys that was next to the coffee table. Gathering some bits of Lego, he said, 'Granny, do you remember when Scruffy ate most of my Lego house?'

'I'll never forget that,' Granny replied. 'The vet charged a fortune and Scruffy's been afraid of Lego ever since.'

Lego wasn't helping Robert feel better about Scruffy, so he put it back and took out a little aeroplane. The tail was all bent, and it reminded Robert of when Scruffy walked round the room with the aeroplane, chewed it a bit, and growled when Robert's dad tried to grab it from the dog, before Scruffy let go of the aeroplane when Granny distracted him with a biscuit.

'I know what I'll do!' Robert announced. 'I'm going next door to ask Mrs Gibbons for my helicopter, the one you gave me just before Scruffy ran off.'

'Sorry, Robert, that's something I had forgotten about,' Granny said. 'Are you sure you want to go there? Maybe I should go instead. She does seem a bit weird, and she shouldn't have shouted at you that time before. Don't you find her scary?'

'Well, maybe just a bit,' said Robert, 'but I'd like my helicopter back.'

Robert mustered up his courage, went out, and knocked on Mrs Gibbons's door. When she opened it, she was wearing an apron with traces of flour and sugar, and had a relaxed, friendly smile. Her pale hair was tied back, as she had been busy in the kitchen, but she seemed pleased to have a visitor. Any nerves Robert felt about asking for his toy were gently wafted away by the kind smell of freshly baked cake.

'Hello,' she said, 'I recognize you, you're the boy from next door!'

'That's right, I'm Robert. I don't live next door. I'm just staying with Granny for a couple of weeks while my parents are at a yoga retreat.'

'Yoga, that's nice,' Mrs Gibbons replied.

'Are you about to say that Beached Octopus is a magnificent pose?' Robert asked.

'I wouldn't know anything about that. What can I do for you today?'

Robert explained that he was there to collect his helicopter, and Mrs Gibbons invited him in. The helicopter was on a side table.

'What took you so long to come and ask for it?' Mrs Gibbons enquired. Then a black cat wandered into the room.

'Your cat's back!' Robert remarked.

'That's right,' Mrs Gibbons said, 'it's Fubbles, he was missing for ages. Then yesterday I went into the garden after we had all that rain, and Fubbles jumped out of a bush. It was like he'd never been gone! Good thing I wasn't working. I was meant to be chopping down a tree and painting a fence for a customer, but when the thunderstorm began I came straight home. I'm a gardener, you see.'

'You're not a witch, then? Only, you wear witches' clothes sometimes?' Robert asked.

Mrs Gibbons laughed. 'No, no. My overalls for work are all black so they don't show the dirt. Sometimes I joke about them being a witch's outfit for fancy dress parties. It's funnier when people see me with Fubbles. So, I got a pointy hat to wear to work and I've called my business "Magical Gardens". I always used to take him with me on jobs.'

'Granny's dog's gone missing. He ran off just after the helicopter landed in your garden. That's what took me so long,' Robert explained.

Mrs Gibbons asked Robert to sit down, and he told her everything that had happened.

'Well, you mustn't lose hope,' she said. 'I gave up far too quickly when Fubbles disappeared. At first I tried really hard. Went round asking everyone if they'd seen him. Asked the police, they were useless. Even tried going back to my old house to see if he'd gone there — he went missing not long after I moved here. No sign of him, and everybody told me to stop searching and just put some posters up, so I did, and got really grumpy for a few weeks. Just when I thought I'd never see Fubbles again, here he is. Maybe if I'd kept looking, he would've been back here sooner. Or maybe not, perhaps it's just one of those things.'

'Granny's been really down. I think she's giving up on Scruffy already.' Robert said with a slow shake of his head.

'It's too soon to give up now!' Mrs Gibbons said, confidently. 'Use your imagination. Think, if you were Scruffy, what would you do, where would you go? You've tried all the normal places. Start thinking like a dog and you'll get some ideas. I'm sure he's looking forward to seeing you again.'

'If I were Scruffy,' said Robert, 'I'd probably be chasing squirrels in the park, but we all walked round there several times and didn't see him.'

'Well, that's a big place for a small dog, so you might've missed him, and tomorrow it's the Craystead Dog Bone Festival in the park. Butchers and pet shop owners from all over the country will be competing to see who has the best bones for dogs! I have a feeling that's where you should look next. Now, I think it's time for you to go back to your grandmother, and don't forget your helicopter, but first I have something for you.'

Mrs Gibbons took Robert to the kitchen, and cut two slices of the chocolate cake that she had just finished icing when he arrived. One slice for him, and one for Granny. 'I made this cake to celebrate Fubbles's return,' Mrs Gibbons said, 'so maybe it will bring you some luck.'

When Robert returned to Granny's, she was watching the news. 'Look at this, Robert!' she exclaimed. 'The newsreaders are in Craystead. Loads of lost cats have suddenly come home. They're everywhere, and nobody knows where they were hiding. What a strange story.'

As if that wasn't unbelievable enough, the next news item made Robert and Granny's eyes grow as wide as the Queen's pizzas.

'That's Scruffy — on the TV!' Robert shouted in amazement. 'He's in the park with the Queen and her corgis!'

'Yes, it is,' Granny added, 'but the newsreaders are saying it ended badly. What on Earth happened?'

*   *   *

'I do love walkies!' said the Queen, as she put her hat on. She'd picked out a bright orange outfit, so she would stand out like a happy marigold in photos of her and her dogs with the grass, trees, and bushes of Craystead Park in the background.

Scruffy had enjoyed his evening in the secret bungalow, where the Queen gave him her last slice of pizza, just before she watched *Casualty*. She was careful to remove the slices of Mars bar, partly because she knew chocolate is bad for dogs, and partly because the chocolate is her favourite part of a pizza.

In the morning, the Queen took Scruffy to Buckingham Palace, where she insisted he have a bath. Scruffy's hair was thick with mud, flour, strands of pondweed, and bits of other debris from his adventure, but once he was in the same room as the royal dog groomer Scruffy smelled shampoo and wouldn't let the groomer near him. The only time he stopped barking was when the groomer got too close and Scruffy tried to bite her fingers. Then Scruffy grabbed the groomer's favourite brush, and chewed it until it looked like a Jelly Baby. At that point, the groomer gave up, and Scruffy was taken outside, where the gardener sprayed him clean with a powerful hose. He still looked untidier than ever, but at least the dirt was gone.

The Queen loaded six of her best-behaved corgis into her grandest Rolls Royce and instructed the chauffeur to drive to Craystead. Barry the bodyguard followed in his Volkswagen, with Scruffy in a safe crate on the back seat. The Queen felt it wise to wait until they were in the park before introducing Scruffy to his new playmates, and she left Crackers at home after his rudeness and sulking the previous day.

When they arrived, the Queen proudly strutted out of the car park, with the well-trained corgis trotting behind her like a hatch of ducklings following their mother. Then she held out a juicy bone, and Barry released Scruffy, who bounded towards Her Majesty like a clumsy hippo.

The TV cameras watched as Scruffy bounced into the air, gleefully swept the bone from the Queen's outstretched hand, and waved it at the corgis like a boastful winner showing off his trophy. The corgis forgot their manners, and yapped in a frenzy while Scruffy galumphed among them. The two biggest corgis ganged up on Scruffy, and grabbed the ends of the bone, with Scruffy in the middle. They jumped in the air and Scruffy let go, then they fought each other for the bone, trampling it into the mud while Scruffy barked. Then Scruffy started bulldozing the other corgis until all the dogs were wrestling each other in a wild, furry scrum.

After panicking for a moment, the Queen did as she always does, putting on a cheery smile for the cameras and waving daintily from various angles. Then the dogs scampered off in various directions, noticing that a number of cats were watching from the surrounding bushes. The Queen marched up to Barry, handed him the corgis' leads and a packet of dog biscuits, which she had been carrying in her handbag, and ordered him to round up the scattered canines while she returned to her Rolls Royce to gather her thoughts. She opened a tin of pilchards for a quick snack.

Scruffy chased a small tabby into the woods, lost sight of the cat but spotted a squirrel, and romped towards the rodent, who disappeared up a tree. Then Scruffy's tail wagged with excitement and he licked his lips: there in front of him stood the stray dog with Scruffy's succulent beef bone, which Scruffy had craved every day and dreamed about each night since his departure from Granny's garden. The stray ran, and Scruffy followed, going deeper into the woods and much further than the corgis could run with their shorter legs.

Barry collected the corgis and bundled them into the Rolls Royce, where the Queen was waiting, then the chauffeur took a long walk around the park in search of Scruffy, but the scraggly-coated beast was nowhere to be seen.

'At least the press and television got some good pictures,' the Queen sighed, 'so perhaps it's mission accomplished. But Scruffy is so adorable! I would so love to keep him in the Palace and take him for more walks. Perhaps I could train him to play snakes and ladders! I was even thinking about having a throne made out of dog biscuits for him, and asking the royal jeweller to make some gold sticks for playing fetch with Scruffy in the Palace grounds, like the royal vet suggested.'

'Ma'am, I do have one idea,' the chauffeur said. 'While I was walking around, I saw a poster. Tomorrow is the Craystead Dog Bone Festival, right here in the park!'

'I'm so glad you saw that poster!' the Queen chirped. 'Scruffy is very keen on bones. Surely he will be there. Let's go back to the Palace, and I shall telephone the festival organizers personally and arrange to attend. Then we shall find Scruffy!'

Chapter 8

'I do love a day out in the park!' Don said, rubbing catnip on a stick. 'And today's the day we make fifty thousand pounds. We just have to find Scruffy first, and get that strange slide out of his collar.'

Ron and Con looked uncertain, but Don was confident. He waited until a dog that was off the lead on a nearby footpath caught his eye, waved the stick, then threw it towards two cats sitting on the grass thirty yards away. Instantly mesmerized by the catnip, the two cats pounced on the stick when it landed, and looked ready to fight each other for it. The dog ran through a flowerbed and on to the grass, colliding with a small bush and uprooting some dahlias on the way. Then he lunged for the stick, and one cat displayed her teeth and hissed, while the other bared her claws and shrieked until the surprised dog retreated. The cats curled up and rolled around, mewing contentedly, while the confused canine strolled off in a sulk.

Don laughed at the animals, and said to his brothers, 'Chin up, it's all going to plan so far. Ron, take a bone and search the woods, while Con and I get organized.' The previous day, the three of them had taken a trip to the coast and robbed a pet shop, taking all the bones and dog treats. Their plan was to set up a stand at the Craystead Dog Bone Festival, as a lure for Scruffy, so they could recover the top-secret slide and sell it to Dodgy Dan, who was due to meet them in the park that day.

Ron headed into the trees, gazing intently around him. It was warm, and for a few minutes he imagined himself as a hunter in the jungle, as if he were seeking an exotic tiger to trap and sell to a zoo. He saw a few squirrels, spotted many cats, and noticed a couple of stray dogs by an old shed. Then he stopped, and smiled broadly: a messy mutt sat just ten feet away, and it was definitely Scruffy. But just as Ron drew breath to call Scruffy's name, he heard an old lady saying, 'Scruffy, it's you! I'm so pleased to see you!'

Ron glanced up to see who it was, and his mouth opened so wide that an aeroplane could have landed in it. It was none other than Her Majesty the Queen, in a bright yellow dress and a hat that looked like a daffodil. Her bodyguard, Sergeant Dobbs, and Constable Cloud were by her side. 'Right,' Ron thought, 'all I have to do is get to

Scruffy's collar, take the slide, and run.' Waving the bone, he yelled Scruffy's name, and the poor dog didn't know what to do. Scruffy took a few steps in Ron's direction, then turned and headed for the Queen, who was also waving a bone. Then Scruffy looked back at Ron, and scampered towards the criminal.

Ron squatted and held out his hands, but just at that moment the most unexpected thing happened. Ron felt a heavy impact on his shoulders and was squished into the mud.

Only minutes earlier, a lady with earrings made of hazelnuts had been standing in the same spot — the same lady as in the accident with Robert's parents — when a hungry squirrel hung out of a tree and grabbed one of her earrings. The lady climbed the branches in pursuit, and was right above Ron when he saw Scruffy. When she recovered her nutty jewellery from the thieving rodent, she lost her grip on the branches, tumbled, and fell on top of Ron.

Ron groaned, and Scruffy ran to the Queen. The next thing Ron knew, handcuffs were slapped on to his wrists, and Constable Cloud escorted him away, while Sergeant Dobbs checked the unfortunate lady was alright and radioed for a first aider to make sure.

Don and Con were completely unaware of what happened in the woods. 'What's taking him so long?' Con asked, once they'd laid out the stolen bones and dog treats on a table at the end of a row of stalls.

'He must be looking really hard for Scruffy,' Don answered. 'Good thing he's making an effort, but let's hope he hurries up. I've just spotted Dodgy Dan. He's early. I'll go and talk to him, and keep him hanging around. When Ron gets back here with Scruffy, send them in my direction. Our little stand will have some customers soon, so sell as many of these treats as you can, but don't sell the best bones before the judges see them. We could win a prize!'

*   *   *

'I do love seeing Scruffy so happy!' the Queen remarked. 'He's sampled so many bones! Which stall is your favourite so far, and have you chosen a winner yet?' she asked the judges, who were comparing notes. Barry and Sergeant Dobbs were still guarding the Queen, but weren't paying much attention to the festival. Dobbs was telling the bodyguard some wild ideas about where all the cats may have come from, but Barry kept his mouth shut about the Queen's encounter with Doris.

'It's a close contest this year, ma'am,' a judge answered. 'The bones on the second stall were particularly impressive. They travelled here all the way from Woofferton in Shropshire. But those people representing a pet shop in Worcestershire had some truly fabulous bones too, they come from a village called Lickey End. There's one more stall left to check out. Then we'll go away and make our decision.'

Con had quickly sold all the stolen dog biscuits, and was counting the money, when he was amazed to see the Queen approaching the brothers' stall. Then he realized that the dog she was holding in her arms was Scruffy. Con gulped like a frog in a sandpit, and thought to himself, 'If I can just make the Queen stand close enough, I can stroke Scruffy's head and take the slide from his collar, nobody will notice, and then we'll be rich!'

'Welcome, Your Majesty,' Con said with his wonky grin. 'Such a lovely pooch, would he like to try a bone?'

'Just a moment, please, ma'am,' one of the judges said sternly. 'We need to examine these bones and make some notes first. Then Scruffy may try one.'

Scruffy licked his lips, and so did Con. Sergeant Dobbs and Barry had their backs turned on the scene, Dobbs making wide gestures and pointing in various directions while explaining his theories about the cats. The judges carefully inspected Con's bones, took some measurements, and scribbled on their notepads.

'Thank you,' one judge said. 'We're all done. Now Scruffy can have a taste.'

The Queen stepped forward, and leaned towards Con, who was dangling a bone for Scruffy. 'Here, boy, get your paws on this,' Con whispered, and extended his other hand to stroke Scruffy's head. But the little dog barked and growled, which drew the attention of Sergeant Dobbs and Barry.

'Hey, you're one of the Three Idiots!' Dobbs bellowed. 'Did you raid another butcher's shop? Barry, I told you about these guys. Help me arrest him!' Con started to run, but tripped over a tabby that was sitting on the grass. Barry pinned Con to the ground and Dobbs put the robber into handcuffs.

'We're not the Three Idiots. We're the Craystead Four, and you'll never get all of us!' Con clamoured, as Dobbs dragged him away.

*   *   *

'I do love a good yoga session!' Mrs Pittick declared enthusiastically to Arnold, who looked extremely bored. 'It's such a shame I'll have to stop now that cat's done a whoopsie on my yoga mat.' They were next to the rockery in Craystead Park, on the edge of the open space where the Dog Bone Festival was taking place.

'I want to climb trees,' Arnold muttered, poking a twig into his nose and wiggling it around.

'You're not going out of my sight,' Mrs Pittick replied. 'Not after what happened on Friday.'

Arnold stretched, yawned, and swallowed a fly that landed in his mouth. Then Sam arrived with a brrrppp of his bicycle brakes.

'What are you doing here, Sam? I thought you were grounded too?' Arnold asked.

'Not me, do you think I'd tell my parents about Friday and risk being stuck indoors all summer? I'm riding round the park looking for Scruffy. Robert and his granny are somewhere over there,' Sam answered, pointing at the festival stalls.

'Mum, let's help out!' Arnold said.

'Alright,' she replied, 'but only if I go with you.'

The three of them pottered past some families that were enjoying a day out with their dogs, and greeted Robert and Granny, who were looking frustrated. 'Still no Scruffy!' Robert sighed. 'I really thought he'd be here.'

'Seeing all these other dogs is making me quite upset,' Granny moaned. 'It's nice to see you here, though, Arnold.'

'He's here with me,' Mrs Pittick said, 'and I'm keeping a close eye on him. We just came to the park to practise yoga.' Arnold pulled a face and stuck out his tongue.

'Is this the bit where you say Beached Octopus is a magnificent pose?' Robert asked.

Mrs Pittick was about to bore the boys with a lecture, when she stared at one of the stalls and her lower jaw dropped. 'Is, is, is that the Queen over there?' she stuttered.

'Yes, it is,' Robert answered, 'and that man she's talking to is one of those horrible men from Friday!'

Mrs Pittick's eyes narrowed and two white spots appeared faintly on her cheeks. 'Is that so? Well, Queen or no Queen, I'm going to give him a piece of my mind!' she exclaimed, and started marching to the Craystead Four's stall. The boys and Granny exchanged some nervous glances and followed Arnold's mother. They got there just as Con was arrested and taken away.

Chapter 9

'I do love seeing the police in action! It seems that man is in the doghouse,' the Queen chortled as she watched Sergeant Dobbs leading Con swiftly out of sight. She tickled the top of Scruffy's head, and for a moment she felt like the whole world was perfect. Then she turned around to an unwelcome surprise.

Standing just yards away, Granny saw her beloved pet in the Queen's arms. Granny raised her arms, and her eyes showed a mixture of shock, delight, and confusion. Granny's jaw dropped and quivered for a moment, then she shouted 'Scruffy!' so loudly that everyone in Craystead might have heard.

'Yes,' the Queen said with a sweet smile, 'this is my dog, Scruffy.'

Don was not far away, and when Granny shouted, he paused his conversation with Dodgy Dan, glared even more stonily than usual, and whispered to himself, 'Did someone say Scruffy?'

Granny scrunched up her face like a sponge, doubling the number of wrinkles in her skin, and the edges of her ears went bright red like two danger signs. 'Your dog?' she screeched, 'How dare you say he's your dog? He's my little Scruffy!'

The Queen stood still, but her eyebrows rose like balloons and she puffed out her cheeks. Granny rolled up the sleeves of her cardigan, squeezed her left hand into a tight fist, and started swinging her handbag with her right.

Barry immediately stepped in front of the Queen and said, 'Don't worry, ma'am, if she gets violent, I shall protect Your Majesty.'

'No!' burst the Queen, brushing Barry out of the way and giving him Scruffy. 'I can handle myself. There are some heavy tins of pilchards in my handbag, so I can do a lot of damage with it if I have to!'

Barry briefly held Scruffy, but the dog leapt to the ground and yapped like an excited toddler. The Queen held her handbag over her head, waving it in circles. 'Scruffy's mine!' she roared.

By now, everybody at the Dog Bone Festival was watching the scene. A local press photographer was rifling through his bag seeking fresh film for his camera, having already taken as many pictures as he'd expected to need.

Don was keenly focused on Scruffy, and was wracking his brains for a plan of action.

Then Sam drew a deep breath and yelled, 'Stop all this, now!'

The Queen had never been spoken to like that before. Taken aback, she and Granny froze and stared at Sam. 'What did you say?' the Queen yelped.

Sam had no clue how to respond. He scratched his curly hair, bit his lip, and opened his mouth, but all that came out was a lengthy errrmmm.

Just then, Robert looked squarely into the Queen's eyes, and calmly asked, 'Your Majesty, you might remember me from the Dog Rescue Centre. I have a question. Are you sure you don't know anything about the lady with the black eye-patch, and the bungalow with the tall privet hedge?'

The Queen took two steps back and winced like a tired boxer on the ropes. Struggling for words, her errrrmmmm was even longer than Sam's. The scene fell silent. Mrs Pittick stared inquisitively at the Queen. Arnold scratched his armpit. Granny stared longingly at Scruffy, who, now aware that something was amiss, sat quietly a few feet away, with his head cocked to one side. Sergeant Dobbs returned from locking Con in the back of a police car, and cheerily asked, 'Did I miss anything?'

Watching from the gathered crowd, Don realized that this was his last chance to act. Turning to Dodgy Dan, he said, 'The slide you want is hidden in that dog's collar. Let's run and get it. Then we keep running, and hide in the woods.'

The criminals launched themselves at Scruffy like a pair of rockets. Everyone was taken aback by the two grimacing figures darting across the grass, but Granny reacted sharply. Before the two men could pounce on Scruffy, she thrust her handbag in Don's face, and punched Dodgy Dan in the stomach. Letting go of her bag, she grabbed each of them by the wrist, twisted their arms, and pushed them to the ground. Then she glanced at Dobbs, who took two sets of handcuffs from his pocket and trudged over. He said to Dodgy Dan, 'Well, well. There really are four of the Craystead Four.'

'I'm not one of those idiots,' Dodgy Dan answered.

'We'll discuss that later,' Dobbs replied. 'You're coming with me.'

'That was incredible! How did you do that, Granny?' Robert asked. Scruffy ran up to Robert, who patted the dog on the head and picked him up.

Granny explained, 'During the war, I was a Senior Commander in the ATS, the women's army. I didn't do much apart from shooting at German bombers, but I was trained in self-defence.'

The Queen stood to attention and saluted. She announced, 'During the war, I too was in the ATS, but only reached the rank of Junior Commander. That makes you my superior officer!'

Granny replied, 'That was fifty years ago. I'm nobody's superior officer anymore. But I think it's about time I took Scruffy home!'

Robert interrupted, squinting at a small, square, flat object, which he was holding up in the air. 'What's this? I just found something odd in Scruffy's collar.'

As they all gathered closer to see what Robert had found, the Queen gasped and declared, 'I think I know what it is. Let me hold it up close.' Robert handed the object to the Queen, and when she inspected it, she nearly choked. 'It has Princess Marina's coat of arms on it. It's the missing slide! I lost this a long time ago, and thought I'd never see it again.'

'If you don't mind me asking, what's on the slide?' Granny asked.

'It's supposed to be a secret,' the Queen answered, 'but just between you and me, it's Princess Marina's recipe for cheese scones.'

'I do love a good cheese scone,' Granny commented, as Scruffy scurried up to her and she proudly fluffed his hair and gave him a kiss. 'Especially when it's topped with slices of Mars bar, an anchovy, and a good dollop of chilli sauce!'

'That sounds like a marvellous combination,' the Queen remarked, and popped the slide into her handbag. 'I'll have to try it sometime.'

Scruffy growled, as another dog had appeared on the scene, a dog that Scruffy had met before. It was the stray with matted fur, who Scruffy had been tracking ever since he was last in Granny's garden. The stray was still carrying Scruffy's succulent beef bone. Enticed by the small pile of bones on the Craystead Four's stall at the festival, the stray waggled his tail and bounced his head, and let go of Scruffy's bone so he could take one of the new treats. Scruffy blissfully bounded to the spot where his beloved bone was glowing in the sunshine, snatched it in his jaws, and returned to Granny with his tail swishing in triumph.

'Now there's a happy Scruffy!' Granny said with delight.

The Queen gazed at the stray, who was busily playing with the pile of bones to select his favourite. 'That's just the sort of dog I've been looking for!' she proclaimed. 'Scruffy is wonderful, but this beast will be the perfect friend for Crackers. A messy mongrel, and he looks so happy and playful. Once he's chosen his treat, he's coming to the Palace!'

'So we can take Scruffy home?' enquired Robert.

'Of course you may,' the Queen answered, 'but on one condition. No more questions about the lady with the eye-patch. I don't know anything about her, of course, but I'm sure she wouldn't like anyone talking about her behind her back.'

Robert agreed, and the Queen took the group to the little shop next to the car park and bought ice-cream for everybody. The Queen chose strawberry flavour for herself, with a drizzle of garlic mayonnaise on top, and Robert and Sam opted for chocolate. Arnold and Mrs Pittick had vanilla, and Arnold fumbled around in his nose and decorated his ice-cream with bogies before he ate it. Granny enjoyed a pistachio cone with a good squeeze of barbecue sauce.

The Queen gave the last bite of her ice-cream to her new pet, and stated, 'It's been a wonderful day, and after that little excitement we can all be pleased with how we've ended up. I just have one more thing to do on the way back to the Palace.'

*   *   *

'I do love a nice surprise,' said Doris. 'It's lovely to see you again, Barry.'

'Her Majesty and I are on our way back to Buckingham Palace after attending the Dog Bone Festival,' Barry explained, 'and there's something Her Majesty wants me to give you. Would you like to step this way for a moment?'

Barry led Doris down her driveway, which looked much tidier now that she had cleared the weeds. Barry noticed that Doris had a new haircut, and her clothes were no longer covered in dust and pet hairs. The Queen wound down the window of her Rolls Royce, and said, 'Good evening, Doris, do excuse me for not stepping out of the car. There is a dog with me in here and I don't want any more mischief.'

'There won't be any trouble, Your Majesty,' Doris answered. 'I feel much calmer now. I even tried some yoga today, and it seems I can still do Beached Octopus even at my age!'

'Wonderful, how does one do Beached Octopus?' the Queen responded.

'Well, you balance on your left knee, put one elbow into your mouth, and your other elbow into an ear.

Your right leg goes over the back of your head, and you put your toes into your nostrils. Then relax all your muscles and let gravity do its job.'

The Queen commented, 'That sounds like a magnificent pose!'

Barry opened the rear door of his car, and brought out a pet carrier he had just collected, with a black and white kitten inside. Doris graciously accepted the gift, beaming from ear to ear, and they said their goodbyes.

As the Rolls Royce went around the corner and up the next road, with Barry's car following closely behind, the Queen was startled when a toy helicopter flew in through her open window and landed in her lap. The dog next to her didn't stir, he was fast asleep after eating lots of biscuits.

'Wait here, driver, I can see where this might have come from,' the Queen instructed.

Stepping out of their cars, the Queen and Barry were greeted by Robert and Granny. Mrs Pittick was polishing a garden gnome, Sam was sitting on the pavement, and Arnold was playing with the worms in his dolls' house on the grass. Scruffy was happily sucking on his bone.

'Does this belong to one of you?' the Queen asked, holding up the toy.

'Thanks, Your Majesty,' Robert answered. 'I thought it landed in the other garden. I was just about to knock on the neighbour's door.'

'Look at this!' Arnold exclaimed, standing up and pointing at the dolls' house, 'It's a palace for earthworms!'

'Fascinating,' said the Queen, 'it's almost as grand as Buckingham Palace!'

Just then, there was a loud brrrppp, and this time it wasn't Sam's bicycle brakes. Mrs Pittick's face went crimson, and Arnold tried his best not to laugh. He imagined that he may have been the first boy ever to fart in front of the Queen. There was a long and uncomfortable pause.

The Queen turned to Barry, and whispered, 'Do you think I should say something?' Barry shrugged. She cleared her throat and said, 'I do apologize for that awful noise.'

'Don't worry,' Sam answered, 'the rest of us thought it was Arnold.'

Granny thanked the Queen for her help with finding Scruffy, and the Queen saluted and threw the dog a biscuit. It seemed the pair had decided to forget that they nearly came to blows just a couple of hours earlier. 'By the way,' the Queen enquired, 'in all the excitement I didn't ask your name?'

'It's Granella, but everyone just calls me Granny for short.'

As the Queen continued the drive through Craystead, her eyes nearly fell out of her head when she saw six cats arguing over a scrap of food. 'Hmmm,' she thought, 'a lot of the animals I released haven't got back to their families yet. Perhaps I'll have to ask Charles to help return them to their homes. He's much better with cats than I am.'

Turning into another road, the Rolls Royce reached the secret bungalow. 'Stop now, driver,' the Queen said. She took the eye-patch out of her handbag, but then she paused and put it back. She thought to herself, 'One does enjoy daydreaming about being an ordinary grandmother, but one has had quite enough of that for now. Perhaps it's best just to be oneself.'

She smiled wistfully, and said, 'Thank you, driver. Now let's return to Buckingham Palace.'

Of course, the Queen still likes to visit her bungalow from time to time. After all, there's nothing she enjoys more than a good pizza.

Appendix
Princess Marina's Cheese Scone Recipe

Ingredients:

8 oz. (225 g) self-raising flour

1 teaspoon baking powder

1½ oz. (40 g) salted butter

5½ oz. (150 g) grated cheddar

5½ fluid oz. (150 ml) milk, and a little extra

3 sundried tomatoes, finely chopped

10 olives, finely chopped

1 teaspoon of mustard powder

A generous pinch of black pepper

A small pinch of nutmeg

Method:

1 Preheat an oven to 220°C (425°F, gas mark 7). If your oven is fan assisted, 200°C (400°F, gas mark 6) should be hot enough. If it often gets hot in

your kitchen, have a fan to assist you with cooling down.

2   Joyfully mix the flour, baking powder, mustard powder, black pepper, and nutmeg in a bowl. Preferably a big mixing bowl, large enough to wear as a hat, but don't actually try it on for size. If you put it upside down on your head with the ingredients inside, your hair will get messy and you won't be able to use the ingredients to make cheese scones, and if you wear the bowl before using it you might end up with hairs in the scones, which simply won't do. It is best to use your imagination and common sense to decide whether the bowl is suitably sized.

3   Add the butter, and mix this in smoothly and lovingly until the mixture resembles fine breadcrumbs. If it helps, have a photograph of some fine breadcrumbs handy, but it is generally sufficient to use your imagination. Having a vivid imagination helps in the kitchen, especially when it comes to baking.

4　Add the cheese, sundried tomatoes, and olives, making soft, gentle movements with your hands until everything is blended well.

5　Dust a light and clean surface with flour and roll the dough to about an inch (2.5 cm) thick. A pastry mat or board is perfect. This certainly shouldn't be done on the floor.

6　Use a crimped circular pastry cutter to cut scones from the dough, and transfer each scone to a greased baking tray. Roll up the leftover dough, flatten it out, and you may have enough for more scones. If you don't have a pastry cutter, it's time to use your imagination again and choose another implement, maybe a spatula or a knife. If using a knife, you should be supervised by a grown up, because (some say) if you drop a knife it is bad luck to pick it up yourself. If you think circles are boring, the scones can be cut in hexagons, squares, or triangles.

7　Once you have put all your scones on the baking tray, use a pastry brush to glaze the surface of your scones with some leftover milk, then put the baking tray in the hot oven.

8   At this stage, give a biscuit to your dog. You have probably been ignoring your canine friend while preparing the scones, so he or she deserves some attention. If you don't have a dog, you have two options: either skip this step or get a dog. The second option is recommended. Dogs are not much help in the kitchen but they make life better.

9   Around seven to ten minutes after placing the baking tray in the oven, take it out carefully, using an oven glove. If the scones are a very light golden brown they are probably cooked, and you can make sure of this by breaking one open to check. The inside should be slightly moist, but not doughy or soggy.

10 Now, give your dog another biscuit. Scones aren't healthy for dogs.

11 Allow the scones time to cool before enjoying them with a little butter, or you can use your imagination once more when choosing what to put on your scones. Chopped Mars bar, anchovies, and chilli sauce are excellent toppings, and there are many other possibilities.

About the Author

As a lover of words, Ewan Pettman was bound to write a book eventually. He likes long words, short words, and even some middle-sized words. His favourite word is 'pilchard'. Eventually cryptic crosswords, Scrabble, and Kan-U-Go weren't quite enough for him, so he wrote *Scruffy and the Secret Life of the Queen*. He hopes you enjoy reading it even more than he enjoyed writing it.